Molly's new school is full of cool girls, just waiting to be her new BFF. All she needs to do is find a way to fit in. Right?

Roseann returned wit[illegible] horts and a heavy wooden stick that curved at the end. "Are you ready?" she asked.

Join in, I thought. *Share the same interests.* Eden would totally agree with my choice to ditch gymnastics for field hockey. My heart soared. I had a feeling that I'd be good at it.

Time to show Roseann what I can do, I thought, eyeing the goal nervously. Tapping the ball to the right, I sprang into a split leap, startling Grace. Ha! I bet she never saw a player do a gymnastics leap before.

Footsteps pounded on the field behind me. Roseann ran up my right side, ready to help. The new Dynamic Duo. I had to make this shot!

With a burst of energy, I sped towards the goal. Fiona ran in to defend it. I heard my stick connect. The ball soared powerfully through the air . . . and far from the goal. My stick kept moving, and I lost my grip.

I watched in horror as my heavy wooden stick spiraled sideways into the sky—right for Roseann's head!

BENDING
OVER
BACKWARDS

More titles in the Picture Perfect series:

#1: Bending Over Backwards

#2: You First

BENDING OVER BACKWARDS

Cari Simmons and

Heather Alexander

An Imprint of HarperCollins*Publishers*

Picture Perfect: Bending Over Backwards

 For information address HarperCollins Children's Books, a division of HarperCollins Publishers, 195 Broadway, New York, NY 10007.

www.harpercollinschildrens.com

Library of Congress Cataloging-in-Publication Data

Simmons, Cari, author.

Bending over backwards / Cari Simmons and Heather Alexander. — First edition.

pages cm. — (Picture Perfect ; #1)

Summary: "Molly Larsen has a plan to avoid being friendless in her new middle school—immediately identify and befriend the IT girl—but Molly's plan isn't foolproof, and her scheme may result in her being embarrassingly branded THAT girl instead" — Provided by publisher.

ISBN 978-0-06-231022-4

[1. Friendship—Fiction. 2. Gymnastics—Fiction. 3. Middle schools—Fiction. 4. Schools—Fiction.] I. Alexander, Heather, 1967– author. II. Title.

PZ7.1.S55Be 2015 2014022026

[Fic] —dc23 CIP

AC

14 15 16 17 18 OPM 10 9 8 7 6 5 4 3 2 1

❖

First Edition

CHAPTER 1

You can so do this.

Mom's first-day-of-school pancakes, which tasted so sweet and fluffy an hour ago, zoomed around like Frisbees inside my stomach.

Any one of these girls would love to be friends with you.

Not if I vomited. Wow, that would be bad. Real bad. I focused on the toes of my new green high-tops. I had to keep it together.

Breathe and smile, the voice in my head said. *You totally own this school.*

The voice wasn't mine. Sure, it was in *my* head, but it was Eden talking.

Eden, my best friend.

Eden, my best friend since kindergarten.

Eden, my best friend since kindergarten, who was back in Arizona.

Without me.

I was here in Hillsbury, New Jersey.

At my new school.

Without my best friend.

Without any friends.

Yet, Eden's voice said. *Soon everyone will be fighting to be your friend.*

That was the plan we'd been crafting all summer long. Eden guaranteed it would work. Pinkie promised me. It felt weird not having her by my side. We do everything together.

Did everything together, I reminded myself.

I was here. At my new school.

But I kept hearing Eden in my head. We'd plotted this day nonstop since Mom had dropped the bomb at the beginning of the summer that we were moving. Every conversation and every plan we'd made at our late-night sleepovers now streamed through my head.

I plastered a smile on my face. Eden says I have a winner smile. I've just got to use it.

I can do this. Just follow the plan.

That was finally me talking to me. I was ready for action.

Sort of.

Taking a deep breath, I watched the sixth graders

push their way through the double doors leading into the Hillsbury Middle School auditorium. They came in groups. Boys with new spiky haircuts and even newer sneakers. Girls shrieking and admiring first-day outfits. Some kids looked happy, others barely awake. Some moved alone, only drawn into the group by the tide.

Loners. I shuddered. It was the very fate I was trying to avoid.

I tried to take everyone in without staring. I didn't want to be that weird girl who stares. I studied the schedule they'd handed me when Mom brought me to the main office. The classroom numbers meant nothing to me. The teachers' names meant even less.

That's fine, I told myself. *Use the paper to spy.*

I held the white sheet in front of my face, pretending I was studying it. I always tell Eden I'd be the perfect spy. Black pants and a cute little black jacket and a fedora tipped low over my eyebrows. My curly brown hair sleeked into a bun. Silver rings on my fingers that are really cameras and telephones and Tasers. I'd go undercover, all mysterious like, to foreign countries and track down stolen data drives or microchips or whatever it was that always got stolen. Eden rolled her eyes every time. She said I'd be found out as soon as I started laughing, which for me is every five seconds.

I have this hiccuplike laugh that always makes people stare.

But I wouldn't laugh if I were a spy.

I definitely wasn't laughing now.

Over the schedule, I spied two girls passing. Both wore the same sandals. One pair black, the other pink.

I gulped, and the pancakes began to bump around again. Eden and I always did that. Bought the same things, but in different colors.

Stop it, I scolded myself. Time was running out.

I'd already been in this school for a full twenty minutes. Eden and I had established that I needed to move fast. Narrow in on the target immediately, before anyone had an opinion of me. Before I got sucked into a bad friendship.

Happy. Smiles. Lots of friends, I reminded myself.

Two girls passed.

"I have to go to the library after school to start," the taller one said. I stared at her rainbow unicorn sweatshirt. Was that the fashion here? I glanced around nervously. Luckily, I spotted no other unicorns.

"Start what?" her friend asked. Her skin was so pale.

"Homework. To get ahead."

Pale girl nodded seriously. Neither girl smiled.

My gaze landed on a group of three girls nearby.

They argued loudly about a music video where this guy with wings dances on a cloud. I'd always wondered too, why the guy had wings, but not enough to get all red-faced and intense about it.

As different girls filed by me, I checked them out.

No, no, maybe, no, maybe, I thought, as if running down a checklist.

Where was she? I wondered. She had to be here somewhere. It was a universal truth that every middle school had her.

There was always an It Girl.

"You're blocking the door. You need to take a seat." A perky woman with cat's-eye glasses placed her hand on my shoulder and gestured into the auditorium.

But—I wasn't ready yet! If I plopped into any seat, who knew what would happen? Eden and I had decided that I'd take charge of my own destiny. Eden's mom was a therapist, and she wrote a blog called See It, Do It. She encouraged her clients to see a picture of what they desired in their minds. By seeing and understanding the picture, you could go out and achieve it. Eden said I should do the same thing. If I became best friends with the It Girl immediately, I'd be set.

Not best-best friends like me and Eden.

Just plain best friends.

The main thing now was to find her.

"Are you okay?" The woman gave me a quizzical look. Her name-tag sticker peeled back slightly from her thin green sweater. MS. FAIRLEY. EARTH SCIENCE.

"Totally fine," I said, more interested in the four girls heading my way. Their hair was so superlong, they could probably sit on it. I wondered if they were growing it for one of those charities that makes wigs for sick kids. Sari did that. She was a friend in my old school. Eden and I went to the salon to cheer when she cut off twelve inches.

The four girls smiled as they talked. They waved to other girls as they made their way down the center aisle. They were liked. My feet itched to follow them. To sit beside them. To ask about their hair.

I hesitated. No. They weren't her. The It Girl.

Eden and I had gone over what makes an It Girl many times.

She is popular. Everyone likes her, and she likes everyone too. She appreciates her friends and wants them to be happy. She's the center of all activity. Plus, she has that special something that makes her fun to be around. Eden and I call it sparkle.

We should know. We're the It Girls at our school.

Well, I was. Eden still is, I guess.

Sparkling without me.

Great.

"You must take a seat." Ms. Fairley gently nudged me into the doorway. Shrieks, laughter, and the rumble of voices rose up as I took baby steps down the center aisle. Ms. Fairley followed. The overhead lights flicked on and off, signaling the start of the welcome assembly.

Ms. Fairley leaned to her right. "Brett, stop kicking the back of that chair!"

My eyes darted to the few empty seats. Time to make a choice. Do-or-die time.

"You have the 'new' look. Are you a new student?" Ms. Fairley nearly bumped into me. My feet had stopped moving.

"Yes. I moved from Ariz—"

I swallowed my words as soon as I saw her. Off to the left, midway down. She'd been hidden by a crowd of girls, all leaning slightly in towards her. But now, as they began to sit, her raven hair shone in the fluorescent lights.

She stood tall and straightened a sleeveless top made from stretchy black material. Her skin still held its beach tan. We'd visited the Jersey shore on our way to our new house, and this girl reminded me of the girl lifeguards in their shocking red swimsuits, sitting confidently atop their lifeguard stands, in charge of the entire Atlantic Ocean.

"Listen, I know this is overwhelming, but I need you to sit now." The teacher's hand was on my shoulder again, this time turning me and guiding me into an empty seat.

"But I—" I tried to stand.

The lights dimmed, and the boys in front of me chorused *"Ooohhhhh,"* pretending they were scared.

"I'll come find you later and show you around. Assembly time." Ms. Fairley blocked my path, and I had no choice but to settle into the seat's nubby fabric.

Maybe this is better, I thought. I can check her out from here. After the assembly, I'll find a way to bump into her. Eden would approve of my quick thinking.

I watched my raven-haired It Girl sit, surrounded by her friends. All I could see was the back of her head, no more than ten rows in front. I twisted the braided silver ring I'd started wearing on my right hand. My dad had bought it for me at a crafts festival. He doesn't do that normally, just buy me something I walk by and like. He says I'm always seeing stuff in stores, in catalogs, online, and asking for it. He wants to teach me responsibility. But this had been our last visit before I moved away with Mom and Alex. He stayed in Arizona with Carmen, his new wife. He probably would've bought me a pony that day if I'd asked.

I liked my ring better. You couldn't bring a pony to school. At least, not here.

"I don't know you," a high, squeaky voice announced, just as the principal took the stage.

"Huh?" I turned my head.

"I totally don't know you," said a girl who sat behind me and to my right. Bouncy strawberry-blond curls surrounded her round face. Freckles dotted her nose and rosy cheeks. Everything about her was tiny except for her smile. She flashed me a wide grin, showing off silver braces. She looked like a cute cartoon character.

How old is she? I wondered. *She can't really be in the sixth grade, can she?* Was she someone's little sister? Was it somehow "bring your little sister to middle school" day?

"I'm pretty good with remembering people, and we had that sixth-grade orientation thingy two weeks ago, and you were not there. Right? You weren't, were you?"

"Nope, wasn't there," I agreed. She wore a purple sweatshirt trimmed in silver studs. I'd had one like it in fourth grade. Now I'd totally outgrown the store in the mall that sold them. But I still kind of liked it.

"That makes you new!" she exclaimed. Her high

voice totally matched her tiny body.

"It does." I twisted back around. I didn't mean to be rude, but laughter floated towards me from It Girl's direction. Ms. Fairley was on them in an instant, and they quieted down. The principal continued his welcome speech. Something about the honor and responsibility of moving into middle school.

I scanned the auditorium, checking for the exit doors. I was pretty confident It Girl and her friends would file past me to get out later. I needed to think of something witty to say. Or funny. Or something.

"Not feeling very friendly, are you? No worries. First-day jitters, I bet. Totally understandable." The girl behind me chattered away. She didn't seem to care that the principal was projecting a presentation on rules onto an enormous whiteboard.

"I'm *very* friendly," I protested in a whisper.

"Great! Me too. I'm Shrimp."

"Shrimp? Like the seafood?" I asked.

"No, Shrimp, like I'm really short," she said.

"Your parents named you Shrimp?" I thought my cousin had it bad when his parents named him Zuza.

"No, silly. It's a nickname. What's your name?"

"Molly Larsen. No nickname." Eden still sometimes called me Mole. She'd started when we were five and they'd read us *The Wind in the Willows* at library story time. The main character was a mole. But I wasn't sharing that nickname. I didn't want to be known as Mole around my new school.

"Hey, Molly, welcome!" Shrimp sounded genuinely glad to meet me.

I gave her my winner smile and turned my attention back to the principal. I'd met Mr. Sabino when Mom registered me two days ago. He'd joked with me then, but now he seemed much more serious. Finishing the rule about respecting other students, he moved on to respecting school property. I wasn't going to write on the walls or stick chewed-up gum under the desks, so I tuned out and watched the raven-haired girl's long hair sway as she stretched. She wore dangling silver earrings.

Maybe I should say something to her about boring rules? Or was that lame? Maybe compliment her earrings?

Giggles erupted behind me, followed by the crinkling of cellophane and the smacking of lips. I turned. Shrimp's honey-brown eyes danced mischievously as she reached up her sweatshirt's sleeve with her opposite hand. "We should shake. You know, to say hello?"

"Shake?" I repeated. What twelve-year-old girl shook hands?

The boy sitting next to me exhaled loudly. "Sorry," I whispered.

"Just give me your hand," Shrimp commanded. The dark-haired girl next to her giggled again.

Tentatively I reached out my hand, and Shrimp grasped it. Then she let go, leaving behind something square and hard.

Back in my lap, I opened my palm and grinned. A Jolly Rancher. And watermelon, my favorite flavor.

"Thanks," I whispered.

"Don't get caught," Shrimp warned. Mr. Sabino was going over the no-food-in-school-except-for-cafeteria-food rule.

"I never get caught," I assured her. Eden and I were legendary for sneaking candy into school. I unwrapped the Jolly Rancher with practiced silence and popped it into my mouth. The boy next to me had no clue.

The screen had now changed to the green-and-yellow school logo, and Mr. Sabino welcomed three students onto the stage. A tall boy with a mop of wavy dark hair, a boy in long basketball shorts, and a girl in a pink polo shirt with a matching pink headband in her long brown hair. Cheers drowned out their names. The entire audience roared for these kids.

"I am pleased to introduce your sixth-grade student ambassadors," Mr. Sabino called out. "These exemplary students were chosen by you to lead you. They are your link to the administration. If you have a problem or concern, talk to them. They will be easy to find, as only they wear the student ambassador green-star pin."

Even from where I sat near the back, I could see the bright green enamel pins on their shirts.

My gaze traveled back to It Girl.

"She's totally pretty, right?" Shrimp whispered in my ear.

"Who?" I pretended I wasn't staring.

"Lyla Silviera. I see you looking at her. How do you think she gets her hair so shiny? I once read you should add egg whites to your shampoo."

"Lyla," I repeated the name. "What's she like?"

Shrimp gave her friend a sideways glance. "You want to answer that one, Sydney?"

Sydney shook her head. "Not so much."

"I'm going to go with . . . popular," Shrimp said. "Lyla is very popular."

I knew it! I just knew it!

At that moment, the lights beamed on, and Mr.

Sabino instructed everyone to head to their first-period class. I glanced at the schedule crumpled in my lap. Social studies in room 108.

"Do you know where you're going? Of course you don't," Shrimp answered before I could. She peered over my shoulder. "I don't really know either. New school for everyone. I'm going to room 314, but I can walk with you, if you want."

Lyla and her friends had already stood and were squeezing their way down their row and into the aisle. This was my chance.

"No need. I'm good. I saw maps posted on lots of the walls," I said quickly. "Thanks, though. And thanks for—" I stuck my tongue out, the Jolly Rancher now just a sliver.

Shrimp stood and stuck her tongue back at me. It was bright blue.

"Raspberry is my second favorite," I remarked.

"I guessed that." Shrimp headed towards the door. "Peace out, Girl Scout!"

"I'm not a Girl Scout."

"Neither am I. It's just a saying I'm saying." She giggled and disappeared into the hall.

Shrimp's nice but a bit strange, I decided. I twirled around, searching for Lyla, who was definitely cooler.

She'd somehow made it across the auditorium and was leaving through the opposite door. I hurried after her.

Time to put the plan into action.

Time to meet the It Girl.

CHAPTER 2

I skidded down the crowded halls, trying to keep Lyla in sight. Her black shirt blended in with the sea of students. As I dodged and weaved, I followed her impossibly shiny hair. Normally I would've been worried about finding my classroom on the first day at a new school. Now I only wanted to find Lyla.

A buzzer sounded, throwing everyone into panic. Clutching their schedules, kids darted right and left.

"That was the warning bell," a teacher called from the doorway of his classroom. "It's the first day, so we understand. Come to me if you're lost." He waved his arms as if signaling an airplane on a runway.

Was I lost? I glanced at the nearby room numbers . . . 165 and 166. I'd made it to the 100s wing, which was good. Ahead of me, Lyla turned a corner and disappeared.

The hallway began to empty quickly, and I sighed.

I'd have to find her later. Right now, I needed to find room 108.

Not knowing where else to go, I turned the same corner. To my surprise, room 108 magically appeared, completely out of numerical order. *Why do schools do this?* I wondered. How could we be expected to learn math or map skills or whatever if the numbers on the doors were totally random?

I stepped inside. WHAT IS SOCIAL STUDIES? was written in red block letters on the whiteboard. Kids wandered about, chatting and catching up on summer fun. Desks stood in a row, and huge maps covered one wall. The windows on the opposite wall were pushed open, letting in a faint early September breeze. I felt myself drawn to them.

Weird, I thought as I headed towards a desk by the window. At school in Arizona, windows were always closed, so the air conditioning could pump. Without air conditioning, we'd melt in the desert heat. Out these windows, all I could see was green—bright green grass and dark green leaves. I never knew the world was so green.

"Oh, Lyla, I love those metallic shoes! Are they new?"

My head whipped around. Lyla? Lyla was in my first-period class!

Luckily, I hadn't sat yet. I left the window and headed towards her. She stood with two other girls near the back of the room. They all compared shoes. Ballet flats. My high-tops suddenly felt totally wrong.

Another buzzer sounded, and a woman with chin-length blond hair and a crisp white button-down shirt cleared her throat. She held what looked like the same red marker that had been used on the board. She was revving up to start class. I had to move fast.

"I saw your silver shoes in a magazine." I pointed to Lyla's feet.

"Really?" Lyla glanced towards me. "Which one?"

I bit my lip. I'd totally made that up. "A back-to-school issue. One of the fashion magazines."

"Metallic is so in," the girl to Lyla's left said.

"Don't you think I knew that, Sasha?" Lyla said. "Diagonal stripes too."

"And red," her other friend added.

"Not dark red. Cherry red," Lyla corrected.

"And denim shirts," I put in. Eden and I had bought them last month. "Really faded ones."

Lyla shook her head. "That was in last year."

"Denim is always in," I said. "I mean, what's not to like about jeans, right?" I gave her a big smile. My winner smile.

Lyla didn't smile back.

No biggie, I thought. *Friendship takes time.*

Then the teacher told everyone to find a desk. Lyla's two friends quickly sat on either side of her. A blond boy slumped into the seat in front of her. My choices were narrowing. I slid into the desk next to him, but I angled my body back towards Lyla.

Close enough, I thought.

The teacher introduced herself as Mrs. Murphy. She read through the class list, and I could tell she'd been teaching for a long time. She managed to pronounce everyone's name pretty much correctly. My name is easy, but others sounded tricky. When she called Lyla's name, I smiled at Lyla.

Again, she didn't smile back.

"What is social studies?" Mrs. Murphy asked the class.

"History," called out a boy near the front.

"Raised hands, please," Mrs. Murphy corrected him. "Yes, but the history of what?"

Lyla raised her hand. "The history of our country."

Mrs. Murphy pointed to a girl by the window. "The history of other places too," she added.

"Yes," Mrs. Murphy agreed, "and no. We will be studying places, both near and far, but social studies

ut people. We are going to be studying human
or over time. We will start right now."

"Don't we need a textbook or something?" the same boy who had called out called out again.

Mrs. Murphy mimed raising her hand, then said, "Not just yet. We'll start by studying the people around us. Everyone take out a pencil and a piece of paper."

I flipped open my new purple binder neatly filled with lined paper. Unzipping the pouch in the front, I found lots of blue and black pens. A highlighter too, but no pencils. I chewed my lip, realizing they were in the new green binder tucked safely in my locker.

Every year since kindergarten I've made a big deal about organizing my school supplies. I love how everything looks so new and the erasers smell so clean. Last night I unwrapped everything Mom and I had bought and laid it on the kitchen table. I filled and labeled my three-ring binders. This year I decided to put all my sharpened pencils in one binder, my pens in another, and my markers in another. Usually my stuff is jumbled and I can never find anything.

New school, new system, I promised myself. I'd never had a system before.

New school and *no* pencil, I realized now. Some system.

I turned towards Lyla. "Hi, listen, do you have a pencil I can borrow?"

"You don't have one?" She gave me an incredulous stare.

"I know, right? Totally silly of me." I laughed. Lyla's eyes widened as I let out a small hiccup.

"Sorry. Don't have one," she said, turning away from me.

I stopped laughing. That was mean.

"For you."

A pink pencil waited on my desk. I swiveled to see who'd given it to me.

"I heard you didn't have one." The girl to my left grinned.

"Wow, thanks." I rolled the pencil on my palm, then squinted at the gold lettering. WRITE ON BLEEKER! "Bleeker? Is this a regift?"

"Regift?" Her dark blue eyes looked confused.

"You know, when someone gives you a gift that they got from someone else. My aunt Kelly used to have a regift party the week after Christmas. It was hysterical. You bring the gift you don't like and rewrap it. Everyone picks one. You just have to hope that the person who picks your gift isn't the one who gave you the ugly thing in the first place. That's what happened to my cousin," I explained. I held up the pink pencil. "Who's Bleeker? A bank? A bookstore?"

"It's me."

"Oh, sorry." I felt my cheeks go pink. "Thanks, Bleeker."

"Roseann. My name's Roseann Bleeker. Mom had personalized pencils made. There's a lot of us, so she only put our last name on them so we could share."

"So, not-so-personal personalization," I teased. "I'm Molly Larsen."

Her face brightened with recognition. "You're new."

"How'd you know?" Could every kid read the newness on me? Was it that obvious? I thought I was doing a good job fitting in.

"You're on the list." She tapped her pink polo shirt, and I noticed her green enamel star pin. "We get a list of the new kids."

Mrs. Murphy started talking about a get-to-know-you exercise.

I recognized her matching pink headband. Roseann was the student-ambassador girl on stage.

"Everyone stand," Mrs. Murphy instructed. Chairs squeaked. "I'm timing you. Exactly one minute. Pick a partner. Go!"

At first, no one moved. Eyes scanned possible

partners. Then, as if an on switch were suddenly flicked, everyone jumped into action, worming between desks to reach their targets. I stayed frozen.

I know no one, I thought, my heart thudding. No, wait, I did. Lyla!

I whirled around and stepped in front of her. This was perfect.

"Hi! I'm Molly!" I said as cheerfully as I could.

"Hey," Lyla said, then turned to the girl to her right. I was left staring at the back of her shirt. Total snub!

Lyla quickly paired up with that girl. The other girl in their trio linked arms with a different girl. I stood nervously in their circle. Lyla acted as if I wasn't even there. I could do the math. I was the odd girl out.

My palms sweated, and I squeezed the pink pencil. Behind me, I heard Roseann's name being called. A swarm of girls and boys surrounded her. Her whispery voice rose above their voices.

Now what? The seconds ticked away. All around me, kids paired up. The plan wasn't supposed to work this way. I should've talked to Lyla by now. I should've, at this moment, been securing an invite to her lunch table. I squeezed the pencil harder. Mrs. Murphy would put me with some other leftover kid. The class would label me as the girl no one wanted.

The pencil gave a *crack*, and I jumped. I stared at the two pieces in my hand.

I gulped. The pencil wasn't even mine.

"Wow! You're strong." Roseann raised her eyebrows at me. She'd stepped out of the crowd and moved to my side.

"I am so sorry—" I began.

"No biggie. I've got tons. My mom had to order one hundred to get a good price."

"I didn't mean to—"

"Do you want to be my partner?" Roseann cut me off.

I blinked, confused. All those kids had come over to be Roseann's partner. What had happened?

"Don't you have . . . ? I mean, everyone came—"

She cut me off again. "You look like you could use a partner." She smiled. Not a pity-the-lost-puppy smile. A you're-okay smile.

"Yes!" I exclaimed.

Other kids grinned at us as we pulled our desks close together. No one seemed upset with Roseann. Everyone liked her!

And so did I.

Roseann lent me another Bleeker pencil. For the next twenty minutes, we filled out a worksheet together.

It turned out we both like the color pink. Our favorite snack is brownies. Extra chewy, not cakelike. None of our other answers matched, but that was okay.

Next we had to walk around the class and introduce our partner to other groups. "Should we go over there?" I asked Roseann, nodding towards Lyla. Maybe if Roseann was by my side, I'd have a good way to start. "Sure," Roseann agreed. Then four other groups hurried over to us. I watched how Roseann greeted each kid as if he or she was the coolest kid in the room. Movie-star treatment, my mother calls it. I glanced at Lyla and remembered how *she'd* treated me.

How could I have forgotten the It Girl trap? Eden and I had talked about it a zillion times. Some mean girls acted like It Girls. Other girls are fooled into thinking the mean girl is the It Girl. Not so. Her popularity comes from kids fearing her, not liking her. Huge, huge difference. An It Girl is truly, totally, majorly liked.

I'd had it all wrong.

Lyla wasn't the It Girl at this school.

Roseann was.

"Molly. Molly? Are you done?"

"What?" I stared down at the homemade pizza on

my plate. My mind was still on Roseann. The rest of the day had gone by in a blur. I'd barely seen her again. "Yeah, sure."

My mom tilted her head. "All good? You didn't eat much."

"The new school is a lot to think about, that's all," I explained. I'd already told Mom all about my classes and teachers. Or at least what I remembered. The first day was only a half day, and we mostly went over class rules and got textbooks.

"I'll finish that." My brother, Alex, reached across the wooden table and snatched the pizza off my plate.

"Hey, that's not your number." I swatted his big hand. Alex is always grabbing my food. That's what happens when your older brother eats fast and you eat slowly.

"I ate your number once before, and I'll eat it again!" His mouth was filled with mozzarella cheese and sauce. I watched him gobble the rest of my number six pizza.

Every year on the first day of school, Mom makes personal pizzas for dinner. She writes our new grade in vegetables or pepperoni slices. This year I had a six made from green peppers. Alex had a twelve made from onions. At the beginning of the meal, we take a big bite into our grade-number pizza, and Mom snaps a picture. When I was in kindergarten and first grade,

I had sauce all over my face in the photo! Mom loves those silly photos. I thought we'd stop with the pizzas when Dad moved out three years ago, but Mom kept going.

"Traditions are traditions because they don't change," Mom had said. Tonight in our new house across the country, she'd made the pizzas again.

But things had changed. A lot.

"I hear you, Molls." Mom rubbed the sides of her head with her fingertips. She was still in her navy work dress, although she'd kicked off her heels as soon as she'd come home. The layers of her reddish-brown hair fell over her tired eyes. "The new job is a lot to think about too."

"But you like it, right?" I asked. We'd moved here for her job. She'd been promised a lot more money and a lot more power to be in charge of advertising for a popular brand of paper towels. Mom had pretended that the move was all about business, but I knew better. I'd overheard her with Aunt Kelly on the phone. She wanted a fresh start. Dad had married Carmen last year, and Mom said she needed "breathing room."

Why did she need eight big states of breathing room? That was what I didn't get. Eight was the number of states between me and Eden. I'd counted.

"I do like it," Mom said. "But it takes time to get used to a new place and new people. And I'm not used to being the boss."

"I'd like to tell people what to do," I said.

"No one would ever listen to you," Alex said. He gulped his water in that glub-glub way he knows annoys me.

"Be quiet," I said.

"La, la, la, la!" Alex sang. Then he smacked his lips together. That grosses me out more than his gulping.

"Both of you!" Mom sighed. "Really now, Alex, you're a senior in high school."

"Molly's in middle school. Don't treat her like the innocent baby," he said. "She started it."

"Oh, please!" I cried. "You just bother me because you have lame friends."

"Molly!" Mom cried. "Stop that!"

Alex doesn't care if I make fun of his red, bristly hair or his smelly deodorant, so I tease him about his friends, because sometimes that bothers him. Sisters know these things.

"Ah, but that's where you are wrong, *Mollster*." Alex grinned in his lopsided way. "All has changed at Hillsbury High."

"Seriously?"

Alex nodded smugly. Mom turned to stare too. Since the divorce, Alex had been really moody. He grunted more than he spoke, and he didn't seem to have many friends. Mom called it a phase and said it would pass. I hoped she was right. I'd never tell Alex, but even with his moodiness, I thought he was pretty great.

"Seriously." Alex pushed his plate away and stood. "The kids here are cool. I'm meeting some of them at the library now."

"Hold up," Mom said. "You need to clear the table before you go anywhere. We talked about this, right? If I'm going to work these long hours, everyone has to do their part."

Alex grumbled as he gathered the plates and glasses.

I tried to make sense of what I'd heard. My shy, unfriendly brother had made friends on the first day. What about me? Had I made friends? I wasn't sure. Roseann hadn't said anything else to me all day.

Mom reached over and ruffled my hair. "It's just the first day, sweetie," she said, as if reading my mind. "Great things are going to happen. You'll see."

I thought about Eden and her mom's blog. I wasn't supposed to wait for great things. I was supposed to make them happen. I was supposed to grab happiness.

"I met this woman at work today," Mom continued.

"She's not in my department, but I saw her in the bathroom."

"You made a friend in the toilet," I teased.

"Yes, my bathroom buddy." Mom grinned. "She said she has a daughter your age in your school. The girl's name is Sheila. How about I arrange a playdate?"

"A playdate?" I cringed. "Alex is right. I'm not a baby. I don't want a playdate with a stranger."

"I thought it would make meeting friends easier," Mom said. "And she's not really a stranger."

"No offense, Mom, but everyone here is a stranger."

"It takes time," she reminded me as she stood to wipe down the table.

I looked at the clock. Back in Arizona, with the three-hour time difference, Eden would just be getting out of school. I thought about Roseann. "Thanks, Mom, but I've got the friend thing covered. Right now, I need to make a call."

CHAPTER 3

All I could think about was lunch.

All morning long, as the teachers began to actually teach, I counted down the minutes.

And I wasn't even hungry.

In first period social studies, Roseann had leaned over and whispered, "Eat with us."

"Okay! Great!" I'd planned to ask her that same thing. Eden and I had worked out how I should say it. Now I didn't have to. Big relief. I didn't know who "us" was, but it didn't matter. I was sitting with *Roseann*.

Now my eyes swept across the huge lunchroom, slowly filling with sixth graders. Roseann wasn't here. Kids jostled to get around me. Standing frozen in the doorway wasn't good, I realized. I wanted to look confident. I had to look as if I belonged.

I joined the line snaking out of the food area. Breathing in the tangy odor, I smelled something with tomato sauce. I groaned and glanced down at my white sweater. I wasn't good with messy foods.

When I'd told Eden how preppy Roseann dressed, we decided I should look the part too. I didn't own any super-preppy clothes. My style was more funky—skinny jeans, colorful shirts with studs or other embellishments, and high-tops. Mom came to the rescue with a cable-knit golf sweater she rarely wore. I paired it with skinny pink jeans, but the sweater was kind of huge on me. Now I pushed up the sleeves. At least my cuffs would be free from stains.

"You have no fear! I like it!" said a familiar squeaky voice behind me.

I turned to Shrimp. "Fear of what?"

"School lunch." Shrimp wrinkled her freckled nose. "Marlo's older sister warned us. Marlo brought a sandwich from home, but my mom's not a sandwich maker. Well, she is, but she smears hummus and cucumbers on pita bread and thinks that's a sandwich. She won't make my favorite. Nutella and banana. She says chocolate spread isn't healthy."

"You like Nutella too?" I squealed. "I make the best Nutella sandwich with cream cheese and strawberries."

Shrimp considered my combo as the line moved forwards. "I'd totally eat that."

We both gazed at the hot-lunch option in front of us. Ravioli drowning in watery tomato sauce.

"Yes or no?" demanded a pinched-face, gray-haired woman. She plunged a big spoon into the vat, sending a spray of sauce onto the clear food guard that separated us. No question. I'd be wearing that sauce.

"No thanks." I slid my tray down towards the vanilla yogurts and bagels. All white foods. All safe.

"Wait! Stop!" Shrimp cried.

I pulled my hand away from a plastic-wrapped bagel.

"I've got it!" Shrimp bounced on her toes. She was always in motion. "Nutella-filled ravioli. Tell me that isn't the best."

"Hot Nutella? Yum!" I agreed, and took the bagel. "But what about the sauce?"

As Shrimp and I both gave the checkout lady our school numbers to pay, she said, "Hot fudge?"

I shook my head. "Too much chocolate."

Shrimp balanced her tray against her hip. I liked how she'd paired a polka-dot shirt with striped leggings and plaid sneakers.

"I know!" she cried. "Strawberry sauce. Then they'd look like the real thing."

"Can you imagine if we switched out the school ravioli with ours?" I asked.

"Hysterical!" Shrimp agreed. "We could—"

At that moment, Roseann stood and waved me over to a table in the center of the room. "See you later, okay?" I said to Shrimp.

"Sure thing," Shrimp agreed. She turned and headed towards a table against the wall. I recognized some of the girls from the assembly. Then she turned back. "Do you want to sit—?"

"I'm good," I said before she could finish. I didn't want her to think I was snubbing her.

"Okey-dokey, artichokey!" Shrimp called. "Wait! How about holy moley, ravioli?"

I laughed. Shrimp sure was silly!

Roseann scooted down to make room for me. The table was packed, but I wasn't surprised. I slid between her and a girl named Miranda, who smelled like oranges and had blue rubber bands in her braces. A tall girl named Grace sat across from us. She tucked her white-blond hair behind her ears and eyed me curiously.

"Do you ride Western?" she asked. "I take horseback riding lessons, but I ride English. Everyone does out here."

"I've never been on a horse," I admitted.

"That's not possible. Roseann said you're from Arizona," she protested. "Don't you live on a ranch?"

"Nope." I shrugged.

"How about donkeys?" Miranda asked. "We rode them when we visited the Grand Canyon."

"No donkeys. Sometimes I rode my bike to school," I offered. "Bikes are much easier. You don't have to feed them, and they don't poop."

Miranda giggled, and Roseann said hi to the teacher patrolling the tables. Grace screwed up her face and asked more questions. She seemed to be having trouble understanding that I lived nowhere near the Grand Canyon or a ranch. She asked about cacti, but what's there really to say about a prickly plant?

Roseann changed the subject from Arizona to a scavenger hunt they all did last week at the town pool. Was she trying to save me from Grace's questions, or had my talk about Arizona been boring?

Nibbling my bagel, I tried to follow along. Something about a missing beach towel and a scoop of ice cream that fell off a cone. And then something about a cute lifeguard.

"Did you see the way Red Hair was staring at you-know-who?" Miranda asked.

"She's so obvious," Roseann agreed, biting into a cheese sandwich. "He didn't care. He's into that girl who teaches the Minnows."

"Did you know the Minnow teacher is going to help when the Eagles practice on Saturday?" Grace asked.

"Oh good!" Miranda clapped her hands. "She's much better than Braid Head."

Minnows helping Eagles? Braid Head? Were they speaking in code? I wanted to join in, but I had no idea what to say.

"Braid Head wasn't too bad." Roseann waved at two girls all in black who passed by. Then three boys said hi to her. I couldn't get over how many kids and teachers greeted Roseann. All different kinds from all different groups. She was the rock star of the middle school.

"That's because you were her favorite player," Miranda pointed out.

"Roe is everyone's favorite," Grace said. She sounded proud of her friend. Not jealous.

"Except Mr. Sabel," Roseann said. "He cringed when he read my name yesterday. He wasn't a big fan of Kate and Lauren, either. Luckily, he liked Chrissy."

I couldn't take it anymore. "Who're Kate, Lauren, and Chrissy?" At least these names sounded human.

"The Bleeker sisters," Miranda explained. "Roseann and her sisters are legends here. The royal family of Hillsbury."

"No, we're not," Roseann said.

"Yes, they are," Miranda mouthed to me.

"How many sisters do you have?" I asked.

"Four. Kate's in eighth grade, Lauren's in tenth, Chrissy's in twelfth, and Jane's still in fourth."

"Is *that* why all the teachers here know you?"

"It would be impossible not to. The famous Bleeker sisters all look alike," Grace said. I imagined a row of five pretty girls with Roseann's long chestnut-brown hair, dark blue eyes, and thick eyelashes.

"And they're all supergood at everything," Miranda added.

"We are not!" Roseann cried. She wasn't being modest. I could see she meant it, and I liked her even more for that. Roseann wasn't stuck up.

Over the next couple of days, I discovered that the Bleeker sisters truly were amazing. Photos of winning sports teams, cast lists from school plays, science fair prizes, and good citizenship awards covered the wall by the principal's office. The sisters owned that wall. They were easy to spot, not only because they all looked alike, but because they all had that same sparkle. I couldn't stop staring at them. Sometimes I pretended I was lost, just to go down that hallway.

Alex was okay as far as brothers go, but I'd always

wanted a sister. Roseann had four beautiful, smart, perfect sisters. She wasn't only an It Girl. She came from an It Family. How cool was that?

As the days went on, all I could think about was Roseann. She'd continued to save a spot for me at lunch. That was good, I knew, but she hadn't texted me at all. I'd texted her twice and she had answered both times, but she hadn't started a conversation.

Don't be silly, I kept telling myself. *Texts don't mean anything.*

"Maybe I'm not exciting enough," I'd told Eden during our video chat last night.

"You are so weird." Eden polished her nails sea-foam green while we talked.

"Not as weird as you!" I teased. "Seriously, though."

"Tell her something about you that will stand out. Be interesting," Eden said.

"Like what? What's interesting?"

"You can gargle water and sing the alphabet," she suggested.

I shook my head. "Not exciting enough."

"You wrote and illustrated an entire book?"

I had, but it was a children's book. A Dr. Seuss–type

thing I did to make Eden's little sister laugh.

"Bigger. I need something bigger," I insisted.

And that's how I came to say what I said the next day at lunch.

I sat at the table with my usual bagel. I'd gotten used to not understanding their inside jokes, but I was picking up on nicknames. The girls called Miranda Flick, and another girl with tons of woven friendship bracelets and a Spanish accent who sat with us was called Striker. I had no idea why.

"The Eagles is our field hockey team," Roseann finally explained. "We all play. Do you?"

"No. I don't know anyone who plays field hockey back home," I admitted. The girls in Arizona were more into volleyball.

They eagerly described the game. Miranda was called Flick because she was queen of flicking the ball into the goal. A striker was a position on the field. Defense, I think. Striker's real name was Anna.

Then all they did was talk about field hockey. About plays. About who made the A team and who made the B team. About a tournament sometime soon in Delaware.

I pretended to be interested. I didn't mention that I hate sports where you have to run up and down chasing a ball. I was the kid who turned cartwheels in the field during T-ball and kindergarten soccer.

Squeezed between Roseann and Flick, I felt as exciting as the colorless bagel on my tray. What had happened to my sparkle?

Roseann's eyes twinkled as she recalled how she and Grace had worked together to score. "They should give gold medals for goals like that." Roseann pointed at Grace. Grace pointed back. Another inside joke.

"I won a gold medal last year," I blurted. "Actually, I've won a bunch."

Roseann tilted her head towards me, suddenly interested. "For what?"

"Gymnastics." I plunged ahead. "I'm a gymnast."

"That's so cool. Are you good?" Roseann asked.

"Yeah." I wasn't lying. I really was a gymnast. And I was good.

"How good?" Grace asked. She liked sports, I knew that.

"Pretty good." I thought back to Eden last night. *Think big. Be interesting*. "I was the best in my gym."

"Wow!" Grace seemed impressed. "So you can do flips and all that?"

"I can. I was working on some really hard stuff before I left." I went on to describe some of the tricks I can do. I told them about the back-handspring contest where I did eight in a row. I would've done more, but the wall got in my way. As I spoke, the energy around me shifted. I had their interest. I had *Roseann's* interest.

"So did you find a new gym here?" she asked.

Luckily, my mom had. "Today's my first day. I'm pretty excited. The next level I'm working towards is huge."

"Big-time huge?" Roseann focused on only me now.

"Very big-time," I agreed, getting into my role in the spotlight.

"Do you mean . . . ? Are you training for the *top*?" Roseann asked, her whispery voice rising.

I leaned back a little, trying to look casual. "I always work to be the best. I'm going *allllll* the way."

"All the way?" Roseann cried.

"TV! You'll be on TV!" Miranda exclaimed.

Wait. What? What was she talking about? I wondered.

"Trials come first, Flick," Roseann explained. "Lots of other competitions too. And training camps, right, Molly?"

"Uh, totally," I said, unsure what she too was getting at.

What camps? Was this another one of their inside jokes?

"We watch the Olympics like crazy people in my house. It's a total obsession," Roseann said.

"Me too," I agreed. "I set up camp in front of the screen when gymnastics is on."

"How amazing is it that you're training for it? I never knew anyone who did that."

"Training for . . . ?" My brain tried to piece together the words, but I was too slow. Everyone began talking at once. About me. About gymnastics. About me going . . . to the *Olympics*?

My mouth hung open. The closest thing I had was a gold medal from the Desert Flower Olympic Festival at our gym in April. But that didn't count. Our local competition was miles—no, worlds—away from the real thing.

Roseann slung her arm protectively around my shoulder. "Chill out, folks, and stop bothering Molly. She's new. She's training for the Olympics. She has a lot going on."

The questions stopped, but not the smiles.

"Gold Medal Girl," Roseann announced.

"Huh?"

"I just came up with that. Isn't it cute for you? Gold Medal Girl." She gave my shoulder a friendly squeeze.

I didn't know what to say. I was conflicted. I'd made myself the center of Roseann's attention, but not in a good way. In a not-exactly-true way.

She tilted her chin towards the trash can. "We should throw away our trash, Gold Medal Girl. Bell's going to ring."

"Listen—" I began, but Roseann was already on the move. I followed her across the lunchroom to tell her she was wrong. I wasn't training for the Olympics. I wasn't anywhere near good enough for that.

Not yet, said a voice inside my head. *But you could be.*

I stopped walking. I'd never considered the possibility. Could I train to be good enough? My old coach did say I was extremely talented.

The bell rang. Roseann waved before hurrying off to art on the other side of the building. I thought some more about gymnastics. I could be really good. I could train for something big if I put my mind to it. I turned the idea around in my head, liking the sound of it.

Molly Larsen, Olympic champion.

I'll wait until tomorrow, after I check out my new gym, to set everyone straight, I decided. *Maybe by then, I'll be training for real.*

CHAPTER 4

"Ready?" Mom asked that afternoon. We stood in front of a huge building and stared at the small sign on the plain metal door: TOP FLIGHT GYMNASTICS. We both were expecting something grander, considering we had heard that this was the best gym in the state.

"Incredibly ready!" I wore my favorite shiny lavender leotard with the rhinestone sunburst design. I'd stretched for over an hour at home, and my muscles felt loose.

Inside I breathed in the familiar smell of sweat and chalk. The *thwack* of bare feet hitting mats echoed off the high ceilings. A girl on the uneven parallel bars on one side of the gym and a girl flying over the vault on the other side stuck their landings at the same time.

"It's enormous," I breathed. My old gym had been half the size.

"I think this building used to be a warehouse." Mom

folded her arms and watched a row of six girls do one-arm push-ups as a tiny woman counted loudly. "This is intense."

"It's great," I assured her. This was the kind of gym that got girls into the Olympics.

"Hello, hello!" A blond man in a navy tracksuit headed over to us. "You are Moll-le, yes?" He said my name with a strong Russian accent. "I am Andre Kamenev."

"We spoke on the phone. I'm Monica Larsen, and this is Molly." Mom reached out her hand.

Andre grasped it between his huge ones, and I thought I saw her wince at his grip. She quickly smiled and asked questions about the gym.

His face was serious. Everything about him was angular, from his sharp cheekbones, to his square jaw, to his wide shoulders. His ice-blue eyes scanned me from head to toe. "Moll-le, your mother says you are a gymnast, yes?"

"Yes," I said. I shifted uncomfortably from foot to foot. I sensed him eyeing my arms. I hoped they looked strong.

"You can do a roundoff–back handspring–back layout? A front handspring–front tuck?" He spoke as if he were barking commands in the army.

I nodded, suddenly unable to speak. Andre was the complete opposite of Daria.

Daria had owned the gym I'd gone to since Eden and I had started there together in first grade. Everything about Daria was soft. Her face. Her body. Her long, red wavy hair. The chiffon skirts she wore. Even her voice.

He's the real thing, I told myself and stood straighter.

"Okay, we try. First you must change," Andre said.

"Change?" I asked.

"You wear this to practice." He handed me a plain red leotard. Only then did I notice that every girl in the gym wore the same one.

"Wait." Mom touched my hand that held the leotard. "Why must all the girls look the same? At Molly's old gym, the girls were encouraged to express their identities."

Daria believed that gymnastics was more than tricks and flips. She wanted us to express who we were with our music, our steps, and what we wore.

"Here the girls wear a uniform. We train my way. Conditioning. Stretching. Strength exercises. All together. The same for everyone." Andre focused his steely gaze at my mother. "We make champions here."

Mom turned to me. "Molly, what do you think?"

She sounded unsure. She had liked Daria and her artistic way.

I didn't mind wearing the same leotard if I could be a champion. "I like red. I'm ready."

"Sofia!" Andre bellowed.

A tiny girl with muscles rippling along her tan thighs hurried across the mats. Her light brown hair was slicked into a tight ponytail. "Hi, Andre!" she greeted him.

"This is Moll-le. Take her to the locker room and then bring her to Nastia's group." He turned to my mom and gestured to a glassed-in space. "So we go over some papers now?"

I followed Sofia along the edge of the gym and through a door against the far wall. The locker room had rows of benches, small metal cubbies, and a bathroom. Quickly I stripped off one leotard and put on the other. Sofia told me she was my age, but she went to a private school. She pointed out different girls as we returned to the floor. "Kelsey Wyant is the best here," she said.

My eyes widened as I watched Kelsey land a double salto with a full twist.

"She's in the top tier. Elite training. You think you'll qualify?" Sofia asked.

Would I? A few minutes ago, I would've said yes. I'd told Roseann the truth when I said I was the best in Daria's gym. Compared with Eden and the other girls there, I was really good. But Kelsey Wyant was a different story.

"I'm not as good as her," I replied. "I'm hoping to get better."

Sofia watched Kelsey with dreamy admiration. "She'll compete in college. Maybe even the Olympics. That's my plan too. I might get homeschooled next year. Andre says I have potential. That's megapraise from him."

"Has Andre ever sent anyone to the Olympics?"

"Of course. Izzy McCabe and Hannah Rice both trained here."

Wow. I had seen both Izzy and Hannah compete on TV.

All summer Mom kept telling me that every cloud has a silver lining. Suddenly I wondered if Top Flight wasn't the silver lining of our move. I'd get really good here. Supergood.

Sofia led me to Nastia, the short woman with a blond ponytail. Her powerful shoulders and thighs told me that she'd once been an elite gymnast.

"We stretch," she said instead of hello.

Joining Sofia and six other girls on the mats in a straddle, I was glad I'd stretched at home. Nastia moved much faster than Daria. Daria had played classical music and allowed us to talk while we stretched. Here the only sound was Nastia's rapid commands: pike, squat, lunge, split.

"Extend." Nastia pulled my leg behind me. Then she pushed down hard on my shoulders. "Get deeper into the split." I cringed, sure my hip bones would crack like a Thanksgiving wishbone.

Twenty painful minutes later, she handed each of us a jump rope.

"What's this for?" I whispered to Sofia.

Sofia raised her eyebrows. "Conditioning." She twirled the jump rope so fast it blurred. With a million tiny jumps, she kept the rhythm.

I started to hum as I jumped. Conditioning at Daria's gym had been dancing to pop music.

"What is that noise?" Nastia asked, coming up behind me.

"I do better with a beat. A melody, you know?" I hummed a few notes.

"No noise," she commanded. "Jump!"

I kept tripping and slapping my shins with my rope as she pushed me faster and faster. My heart was racing by the time we finished.

I glanced across at the parent waiting area. Even

from this far away, I saw the frown lines Mom gets in her forehead when she's worried. I flashed a thumbs-up to tell her I was fine. I just needed to get back into shape.

"Floor warm-up. Do what they do," Nastia said before she walked away. Everything moved so fast here.

I followed the other girls, who lined up at the corner of the large mat. The warm-up started simply. Forward rolls diagonally across the mat. No problem. We went one at a time. Then cartwheels, front walkovers, and then back walkovers.

"Move on up . . . up to the top . . ."

Voices chanted as I did one back walkover after the other. I tried to concentrate on my form. Not only were Nastia and the other girls watching me, but I also sensed that Andre had his eyes on me.

"Wait, don't hesitate . . . move on up . . ."

The chanting grew louder as the first girl began back handsprings. I couldn't believe the height she got.

"Dominate . . . intimidate . . . move on up . . ."

Was it someone's floor routine music? It was catchy, but I'd never heard anyone use anything with chanting.

"What's going on?" I whispered to Sofia, who waited in front of me.

"The cheerleaders." Sophia pointed to the wall

behind us. "The building is divided in two. The other side is Top Flight Cheer. The wall doesn't go all the way up. Andre said it has something to do with air flow."

I noticed that the cinder block wall stopped several feet before the ceiling.

"They're awfully loud." I tapped my foot in time with their chant.

"And annoying. We share the locker room with them." Sofia scowled.

"You don't like them?"

"Of course not, they're cheerleaders. You know what *that* means." She stepped to the edge of the mat, readying herself to start.

"What?"

"They weren't good enough to be serious gymnasts like us." Sophia began her series of back handsprings.

I couldn't hold back my gasp. Sofia's back arched perfectly as she launched into each flip with incredible power. In seconds, she'd covered the length of the mat. She was good. Crazy good. Everyone here was.

"Move on up . . . up to the top." I chanted along under my breath as I began my turn.

CHAPTER 5

I grasped the banister as I crept down the stairs the next morning. If I let go, I feared my body would slump and I'd tumble. My arms throbbed from push-ups and handstands. My legs burned from squats and extensions. Even my toes ached from gripping the mat. Last week, Mom yelled because I kept sliding down our curvy banister. Now I was hobbling worse than my great-grandmother!

I'll stretch as I bake, I told myself as I entered the dark kitchen. The clock on the microwave read 6:22. I was never up this early.

I padded quietly in my blue fuzzy slipper socks, hoping Mom wouldn't hear. The gurgling in the pipes told me she was already in her shower. Alex needed a fire truck to wake him. I pulled out the box of brownie mix and the oil from the pantry. In the cabinet, I found a bowl and a wooden spoon and got to mixing.

I was good at making brownies. I was even good at cracking the egg.

As I waited for the oven to preheat, I lifted my phone from the charging station on the desk. I'd been too wiped out last night after gymnastics to check my messages. I wasn't surprised to find one from Eden.

> 411 on new gym? Did they luv u? they must b stoked 2 have star like u!!

I swirled my finger in the batter, then licked it. Eden thought I was great at gymnastics. She hadn't seen the girls at Top Flight. She hadn't heard Nastia list all the things I do wrong. She didn't know how my body hurt this morning.

> U wont believe how bad

I started texting but stopped. Gymnastics was the one thing I'd always done better than Eden. Eden got better grades. Her hair always blew out glossier and straighter. Eden's parents were still married and even held hands when they watched a movie. Plus she had two adorable little sisters who idolized her. But I was the gymnastics star.

The move had messed me up and gotten me out of shape, I decided. With time, I'd be the star here too. A superstar!

I began again.

> totally awesome!!! way better than Darias!

"What are you doing?" Mom demanded.

I whirled around. "Baking brownies."

"I can see that, Molly. Hear all the clanging too. Why, may I ask?" Mom tried to sound angry, but I could tell by the way her lips turned up that she found it kind of funny that I was in my pajamas baking so early.

"Today is Sweets Friday. Not for the whole school. Just our lunch table. Roseann made it up. Every Friday we're going to bring a sweet snack to share," I explained as she helped me slide the pan into the oven.

"That sounds nice." Mom rummaged in her leather work bag. "You've found friends so fast."

"I did." I knew Roseann would be happy that I'd remembered she loved chewy brownies. Best friends remembered things like that. "Need this?" I asked, pulling her work ID badge from under a dish towel.

Mom sighed. "Yes. This house is a mess, and I have

no time. I need to leave for an important early meeting."

"What about me?" I'd been planning on Mom dropping me at school. I could walk, but I was too lazy in the mornings. Plus, today I had the brownies.

"A woman I work with is picking me up. I'm leaving the car for Alex to drive you." She grabbed a pear from the fruit bowl as a car horn honked. "I woke Alex. Tell him there's a list of chores on the fridge. He needs to do his, and you need to do yours. Got it?"

"But Mom—"

"I'm sorry, sweetie. I've got to go. Have Alex help you with the oven and remind him to pull up the weeds by the mailbox. It's weird having grass all over our front yard, isn't it? Next up is fixing the backyard." She kissed me on the forehead, then left.

I stretched out my sore legs as I licked the last of the batter off the spoon. Back home, Mom would brew coffee and have breakfast waiting when we woke. Then she'd drop us at school on her way to work as we listened to her favorite country-western station. Even after Dad moved out, the mornings had stayed the same.

We'd lost our routine here, I'd realized. I guessed we'd have to find a new one.

"Are you kidding me?" Alex shuffled into the kitchen

in jeans and a faded polo shirt. His dark red hair stuck up where he'd slept on it. "Why aren't you dressed?"

I pointed to the oven. "I'm baking brownies."

"Now? I need to get to school to get a parking space. Hurry up and get dressed."

"We have plenty of time." I slid gracefully into a split.

"I'm leaving," Alex warned.

"Mom wants you to weed," I called as I headed up to my room.

Alex grumbled, and he was still grumbling when I came back down in my white jeans and bright green shirt. He shook the car keys. "Out the door."

"The brownies have five more minutes to bake," I protested.

"Too bad. I'm not waiting." He slung his backpack over his shoulder and headed into the garage. I heard the garage door rise.

I had no choice. I turned off the oven. *Roseann likes chewy brownies,* I reasoned. These would be extra chewy.

Alex beeped the car horn. He was serious about leaving.

I slipped my backpack over both shoulders, then pulled on two of Mom's flowered Vera Bradley oven mitts. I slid the steaming pan from the oven. *The brownies can cool on the way,* I decided. *I'll open the windows. The breeze will help.*

Carefully I shimmied into the car. "Buckle me in, okay?"

Alex rolled his eyes but leaned over and helped. "Leave the baked goods behind. You'll burn yourself."

"No way. It's Sweets Friday."

"Make it Salty Friday. Bring pretzels. Who cares?" he said.

"I do. The treat has to be sweet. It's Roseann Bleeker's idea. Her sisters used to do it when they were in sixth grade."

"Bleeker?" He backed out of the garage and stopped at the end of our driveway. "Bleeker?"

"Yes, Bleeker. She's my . . . new friend." I wanted to say best friend, but that wasn't right. Not yet.

Alex gazed out the windshield, deep in thought. "She has a sister. My year."

"She has lots of sisters, so? Are you going to drive? My arms are starting to kill from holding up this pan."

Alex twisted around and snatched his thick math textbook from the backseat. "Put this on your lap, then rest the pan on it."

"Thanks." I did what he said. "What's with the caring?"

Alex shrugged and drove down the street. "Her sister is cool. Really cool."

"Ooh, you like her!" I sang.

"Every guy likes her. I've just seen her, that's all."

I zipped my lips, even though it would've been so easy to tease him. Alex has never had a girlfriend, and he hates it when my dad tells stories about all the girlfriends he had in high school.

I felt bad for Alex. He was shy, and I was sure Roseann's beautiful sister was way out of his orbit.

"How am I supposed to carry these in?" I asked Alex, tilting my chin at the heavy metal pan balanced on the book in my lap. There was no way I was entering middle school wearing flowered oven mitts on my hands!

"You have the craziest problems, Mollster."

"I know." I sighed. Dad always said I plunged into things without thinking about them.

"There's a brown bag in the back. Mom bought something at the hardware store." At the next stop sign, he grabbed it for me. Talking about the Bleeker sisters had certainly made him less grumpy.

I pulled a hammer and a wide putty knife from the bag. I struggled to hold the knife with my big oven-mitt hands. "Presto! It's now a spatula." I stabbed it into the warm, gooey brownies and sliced them into jagged squares.

Using my fingers, I scooped the squishy brownies into the brown bag. Chocolate smeared on my hands and on the outside of the bag. Just as I pushed in the last one, Alex pulled into the school's drop-off lane.

"You're making a mess," he said, inching the car forwards. A burly gym teacher waved us on.

I wiped my hands on the oven mitts. I licked my wrists. Chocolate smudged on the leather seat.

"Paws off the car! Mom will go nuts." Alex stopped by the curb.

I squirmed. Sitting with the backpack had made my shirt ride up and given me a wedgie. The gym teacher motioned to me, but I wasn't getting out like this.

"You're holding up the line!" The teacher knocked on the window.

I pretended not to hear him. Placing the pan of brownie bits on the floor, I unbuckled my seat belt and straightened my clothes.

"Move it, Mollsters." Alex nervously eyed all the cars waiting behind us. He was still pretty new at driving.

I tried to balance the warm bag of brownies as I opened the door and stepped onto the sidewalk. With one hand, I smoothed my pants again.

"Wait, Molly, you—" The teacher slammed the door, cutting Alex off. Alex pulled away, and I had no idea what he'd been trying to say.

The first warning bell rang, and I hurried to my locker. The paper bag sagged from the heat building up inside. I had a bad feeling the brownies were congealing into a huge blob.

The halls emptied. Kids ducked into their first period classes. I placed the bag on the floor by my feet. Then I did battle with my lock. Right, left, right. Nothing. I always needed at least three tries to open it.

"Ewwww! You didn't!" shrieked a girl behind me.

Another girl giggled loudly.

I had only seconds before class started, so I kept twirling.

"Molly, maybe you want to use a bathroom?" Lyla slid up alongside me and pinched her nose with her fingers. Two of her friends folded over in giggles.

"What?"

"You—" Lyla covered her mouth, then burst out, "You pooped your pants!"

"What?" I twisted and saw streaks of brown across the backside of my white jeans. "No! You've got it wrong!" My face flamed. "It's brownies."

They wouldn't stop laughing and holding their noses.

"It's not what you think!" I stepped forwards to show them. A loud *splat* made me cringe. The paper bag tore as I stepped on it. Warm brownie mush splattered across my green sneaker.

"Ew! Gross!" Lyla and her friends shrieked.

Mrs. Murphy raced out of the classroom. She sized up the paper bag and the mess on my pants. "Oh, dear. Oh, dear," she repeated, shaking her head.

I cringed. Did she think I carried my dog's poop to school?

"It's brownies, I swear!" I cried. I reached down to prove it to her.

Mrs. Murphy shooed Lyla and the other girls into the classroom. She turned to me. "Molly, honey."

And as I squatted on the floor, next to the bag of brown mush, Roseann appeared in the empty hallway. She held a late pass. She stared at me, her eyes wide in surprise.

"It's funny, right?" I said. I so wanted to cry, but I smiled instead.

"Roseann, just the person I need." Mrs. Murphy turned to me. "Molly, why don't you leave that and I'll call the janitor? Go with Roseann to the bathroom to get cleaned up."

"I'm fine. I don't need help." I wanted to see the damage by myself.

"What about her pants?" Roseann asked.

Mrs. Murphy's eyes darted to my backside. Roseann looked too. I tried not to melt into the floor.

"That's a problem," Mrs. Murphy agreed. "Can your mom bring—"

"She has a big meeting at work," I said.

Mrs. Murphy nodded. She was a mom too. I'd seen a picture of her toddler son on her desk. "Roseann, detour to the nurse's office and see what she can dig up for Molly."

I hurried into the girls' bathroom. Luckily it was empty. Cleaning off my sneakers was no problem. I soaked a wad of paper towels with water and rubbed my pants. The chocolate smeared even more.

Now my butt was brown *and* wet!

"This is all she had in lost and found." Roseann pushed open the door and held up an enormous pair of black sweatpants. The words UGGA BUGGA were printed in red down the left leg.

I groaned.

"You can't wear these," Roseann said. "They're gross."

"Do I have a choice?" I took the sweatpants from her. "They were brownies, just so you know."

"I believe you."

"Thanks for helping me." I was glad Roseann was here. Just the two of us.

"It's fine." She leaned against the sink.

"They were for Sweets Day," I called from the stall where I peeled off my stained white pants. "Extra chewy and gooey," I said in a funny voice.

I expected Roseann to laugh. She didn't.

"Wow," she said as I modeled the clownlike sweats. "That's bad."

Next to Roseann in her crisp plaid shorts and matching baby-blue shirt with the green star pin, I looked beyond silly.

"What will people say?" She seemed concerned and nervous for me.

I shrugged. "Ugga Bugga?"

That made her smile. We walked back to class together.

All day when kids called out "Ugga Bugga," I never stopped smiling. Dad always told me it's important to know when to laugh at yourself. Even in those dumpy sweatpants, I knew the brownie-poop thing was funny.

But I wasn't sure Roseann knew that.

I thought about one of the It Girl rules Eden and I had come up with over the summer. *Don't be the embarrassing weird girl.*

Too late. I'd done that today.

Tomorrow I'd try harder. Roseann and I were on our way to becoming friends. I just had to make sure I didn't do anything else to scare her off.

CHAPTER 6

"That is too hysterical!" Eden cried. The sides of her eyes crinkled when she laughed.

"Sure, that's really funny, isn't it? You didn't have brownie on *your* butt." I tried to sound angry, but I wasn't fooling Eden. Even on the computer screen, she could see my cheeks puff as I held in my giggles.

"I know." Eden suddenly turned serious. "I wish I was there. No, I wish you were here." She picked the cuticle of her thumbnail. She always did that when she was worried. "Don't sweat the brownie thing. Roseann sounds cool. She'll roll with it."

I rested my chin in my hand and stared at Eden. If I reached out, I felt as if I could touch the heart charm she always wore around her neck. But if I tried, my fingers would hit the computer screen. Video chat was amazing, but it was also a cheat.

I adjusted my laptop on the metal table on our

patio. The very beginnings of yellow and red had crept into the leaves on the trees that lined our backyard. I'd never seen the seasons change before. I wondered what our yard would look like in a month. Back where Eden was, it was still too hot to sit outside in the middle of a Saturday in September.

"You need to move on." Eden was all business now. She twirled a strand of her sun-streaked hair. "You and Roseann are really close to bonding. I sense it."

"From there you can sense it? Do you have superpowers?" I teased.

"Definitely! I'm Superbestie! I control friendships. I make them! I break them!" Eden flipped her zip-up sweatshirt into a cape. "My power puts fear into girls everywhere!"

I cracked up. Eden and I can always make each other laugh. "So why aren't you working your magic on me, O powerful BFF?"

"Ah, but I am. I have your next assignment." Eden squinted and leaned into the screen. "Hey, are you listening to me?"

"Yeah, just checking my phone, that's all." I tucked my cell in the pocket of my jeans. "Roseann might text."

"Really? That's great!" Eden sounded excited.

"Yesterday, even though I was wearing those

hideous sweats, Roseann and the girls at lunch talked about getting together for fro yo today," I explained. "They might go after their field hockey practice. Or maybe it's a game. I don't know. She's supposed to text."

"You totally need to go," Eden said.

"If she texts." I was having trouble reading Roseann. Eden was so animated. I never had to guess how she felt about anything, especially me.

"So I made a list." Eden held up a piece of notebook paper covered with her handwriting in purple pen. "The next step is to join in more."

"Join how?"

"My mom tells women looking for boyfriends that guys like girls who have similar interests. It gives you something to talk about and do together. I think it works for friends too. Don't you?"

"I guess." I leaned back in the metal chair and wondered what Roseann and I could do together.

A flash of yellow through the trees caught my eye. Then it was gone.

"You said she does a lot of stuff in school. Clubs and teams." Eden's voice floated from the computer, but I'd stopped looking at the screen.

The yellow flew by again, then disappeared. What was it? Did they have big yellow birds in New Jersey?

"Moll? Yoo-hoo?" Eden called.

"One sec." I needed to confirm my Big Bird sighting. I twisted to see better past the corner of our fenced-in yard. The yellow blur flew into sight again. This time I noticed a reddish color too. I stood, and it was gone.

I stepped off the patio. The yellow twisted through the air. A body, not a bird.

A girl, I decided. A girl who could fly!

"Hey, let me call you right back. I have to see something!" I yelled towards the laptop.

The fence that surrounded our yard was twelve feet tall. Bushes and shrubs grew around it, covering the solid brown wood. Every house in our neighborhood had one. You couldn't see into anyone's yard. Mom liked the privacy.

The yellow girl somersaulted through the air, then disappeared.

So weird.

She flew back up. Legs outstretched in an impressive split.

I took a step towards where the fences of four houses met in a corner. The flying girl whizzed up. As she launched into another split, our eyes met.

I knew her!

I waited, but she didn't soar up again.

“Molly? Is that you?” a squeaky voice called from the other side of the fence.

“Shrimp?” I cried. The fence was too tall to see over. “Where are you?”

“Here.” Her voice came from the yard diagonal to ours. “I live here.”

“I live over here. How were you doing that? The flying thing?”

“It’s a trampoline! I’m practicing.”

“Practicing for what?” It was strange talking to someone I couldn’t see.

“Cheerleading. I’m a flyer on a competitive cheering team.”

“What’s a flyer?” I sat on the patchy grass near the fence.

“I’m the top of the pyramid. I stand on shoulders and do flips off. I’m the flyer because I’m tiny.”

“Really? You’re short? I never noticed,” I teased.

Shrimp laughed. “I can see how you wouldn’t notice. My gram says my personality is bigger than my body. That’s a good thing, by the way.”

I told her about training at Top Flight. Turned out, she was at Top Flight Cheer, just around the wall!

“Shhh!” she warned, and lowered her voice. “My little brother is coming. I don’t want him to see you. I love freaking him out. This'll be fun. Play along."

Uh, okay. I pressed my lips together and heard footsteps approach through the grass. "Who are you talking to?" a boy asked. His small voice grew louder as he ran over.

"N-n-no one." Shrimp sounded frightened. "I mean, it's a secret."

"Tell me!" the boy cried. He sounded about six or seven. "I won't tell Mom this time."

"I don't want to scare you, C.J. It's safer if you don't know."

"You can't scare me," C.J. insisted.

"Really? Okay." Shrimp paused. "There's a ghost in that prickly bush by the fence."

I heard C.J.'s footsteps move closer. "Where?"

"Whoa, stay away!" Shrimp cried. "It's an angry ghost."

"How'd you know?"

"Watch what happens. I'm going to take this little pink ball . . ." I grinned as Shrimp spoke. I knew what she was planning. "And I'm going to count to three, then throw it. One . . . two . . . three . . ."

The ball thwacked against the leaves and the fence.

"Oohhhh!" I groaned in my deepest, spookiest voice. "Who goes there?"

"What's that?" C.J. sounded scared.

"I am the Ghost in the Bush. W-w-why have you woken me?" I boomed.

C.J. gulped loudly.

"Help me! Help me get out!" I bellowed in a creepy voice. "I'm trapped! *Ohhh* . . ."

"Mom!" C.J. cried.

"Hey, scaredy cat, it's a joke. Relax. There's no ghost." Shrimp laughed. "It's Molly."

"Who's Molly?" C.J.'s voice quavered.

"I am the Ghost in the Bush," I moaned.

"I'm telling! Mom!" His footsteps pattered away as he ran off.

"That was excellent," Shrimp choked between giggles. "He was totally shaking."

"Is he okay? I don't want to get you in trouble," I said.

"He's fine. He likes being scared. He says he doesn't, but he does. Mom will lecture me, but it was so worth it. And you knew exactly what to do."

"You set it up great," I said. "It was like we planned it."

"Classic! Hey, do you want to come over?"

At that moment, my phone buzzed. I slid it out of my pocket.

@ Swirl Fro Yo on Tucker St in 20 min.

Roseann! I wanted to hang with Shrimp, but I wanted to hang with Roseann even more.

"Can we do it another time?" I asked. "I have plans."

"Sure, no prob, Ugga Bugga!"

"You know about that?" I cried.

"Who doesn't? Why were you bringing brownies to school anyway?" Shrimp asked.

"Long story." I groaned.

"Tell me later, okay? I'm going back to my trampoline. Out the door, dinosaur!"

"See you!" I called as I ran into my house. In my mind, I worked on ways to beg Alex to drive me to town. He hated chauffeuring me around. I knew he'd complain, but I planned to trade him for some of his chores. I had to see Roseann.

And I had to text Eden.

Our plan to be friends with the It Girl was finally working!

CHAPTER 7

"You look like a wet noodle!" Andre shook his head in frustration.

I swallowed hard and tried my back walkover on the beam again.

Tighten up, I silently commanded my legs and my stomach.

"Stop! Stop!" Andre cried as my feet touched down in a perfect line on the four-inch-wide beam. "Floppy! Why are you so floppy? Like a rag doll!"

"I don't know." Daria had never called me floppy. She said our bodies had to flow.

"Again! Again!" Andre folded his arms. "You have a lot to correct."

"Correct?" I'd only been at the gym for an hour and a half, and already my legs were trembling. He'd had me do vault and now beam. Over and over.

"Everything is wrong. Your feet are too flat."

Andre continued to list all the parts of me that weren't working—my extension, my posture, my landings. Pretty much everything.

My eyes searched out Sofia. She practiced her leaps alongside the beam, waiting her turn. I shot her a pleading look.

She shrugged and kept on leaping. Each one higher than the one before. Her toes pointed gracefully.

I looked around at the other girls in my group. They'd been friendly earlier in the locker room, but out in the gym, they were all business. No one gave me thumbs-up or an encouraging smile. Each girl concentrated on only her own moves.

Gymnastics had never been lonely at Daria's gym. I missed Eden and the others cheering me on. Even when they did it silently, I knew they were rooting for me.

I was on my own here.

Andre had me do that back walkover twenty-two more times. I didn't give up. No matter what he said, I stayed strong.

I just wished he'd said something nice. Anything.

"Back tuck dismount," Andre called. "You can do this, no?"

"Sure," I said. I'd do a flip any day. Especially a

backflip! I hated the slow, stiff moves where I had to point my toes.

I turned a cartwheel, and as my feet hit the beam, I sprang backwards into the air. As my feet landed solidly on the floor, I raised my arms.

I looked expectantly at Andre. I knew that was good.

"Body rounder in the tuck this time," he said.

My shoulders slumped as I climbed back onto the beam. Daria always said something nice, even if she had tons of corrections to make. How good would I have to be to get praise from Andre?

"That's the way, Kelsey!" he called across the floor as I landed my second back tuck. I lifted my head in time to see Kelsey nail an amazing double salto. This girl was good enough to be on a cereal box!

That's *what it takes*, I thought. I hopped onto the beam again, ready to work harder. I could win Andre's praise.

But by the end of the evening, he had bumped me down a group!

"But . . . but—" I sputtered. How could I be moving backwards?

"First you must fix your positions. You are strong, but you are sloppy." He handed me over to Nastia's group.

"He knows what he's doing," Sofia whispered to me

later, as we stretched for our cooldown.

"My old coach thought I was ready for your level."

"Did your old coach make champions?" Sofia asked.

I'd always believed Daria was the most fantastic coach. We'd had so much fun working out at her gym, putting on random music and making up tumbling routines.

"No," I admitted. Daria made us smile, but she didn't make champions. She didn't care about perfect body positions.

"You'll tough it out. We all do," Sofia said as we opened the locker room door.

Screams and laughter hit me like a tidal wave. The gym floor had been so quiet with all the girls concentrating on their moves. The locker room sounded like a slumber party after midnight when everyone was loopy with sugar.

"What's going on?" I asked.

"Cheerleaders." Sofia grabbed my hand and pulled me into a corner. "They change on that side. We change over here."

Other girls in red leotards hurried to pull on their warm-ups and slip on shoes.

I couldn't help watching the cheerleaders. They all wore cheer shorts in different bright colors and cute tank tops. I loved one in purple zebra print and one that spelled CHEER in magenta sparkles.

The cheerleaders talked about TV shows and websites. They seemed in no rush. The gymnasts were too tired to talk. We all wanted to go home and collapse. At least I did.

"Think fast, Molly!" Shrimp popped up from behind a bin of sweaty towels and hurled one in my direction.

I ducked. "Gross!" Then I flung it back at her.

Shrimp squealed as it hit her white sneakers. "Hey!"

"You started it!" I realized I hadn't seen Shrimp in school today. We didn't have any of the same classes.

"I did," she agreed. Shrimp picked up the towel and wiped sweat from her forehead. Her curly hair was pulled into two short braids. She looked cute in black Lycra shorts and an orange racer-back tank. "How was practice?"

I groaned. "Fine."

"You sound like you went to the dentist or had to take a science test."

"It's hard," I explained. I glanced at Sofia. "The coaches expect a lot."

"You should try cheerleading," Shrimp suggested. "Right, guys?"

"Woo! Yes! Come cheer!" the girls near us all yelled.

"No way," I scoffed. "I'm a serious gymnast. We tough this stuff out."

Sofia reached over and slapped me a high five. "Serious gymnasts rule."

"Totally," I agreed.

"Have fun being serious!" Shrimp grinned as if I'd told a joke.

Was it a joke? I wondered. Could I do this?

I'd never been a serious gymnast before. I'd never been a serious anything before. Seriousness didn't come totally naturally to me, I guess. But I had to try. My entire "new girl" plan was riding on it!

I spent all my time thinking about the Roseann Project. That's what Eden called it when she was trying to sound like her mother. She planned to be a therapist too when she grew up. She always fixed, or tried to fix, our friends' problems, so she'd be good at it.

Roseann and I were getting on great. I no longer had to rush to lunch, because there was no question that I had a place at her table. Miranda, Grace, Anna, and all the other girls greeted me in the halls. Miranda offered to hold my feet when we did sit-ups in gym. We all hung out on the benches outside the frozen yogurt place on Saturday, comparing toppings.

And that was the problem.

The group thing.

Roseann always had a group around her. If not the girls from lunch, then boys who had crushes on her or girls who needed help with their homework or kids who just wanted to be near her. She radiated an energy that drew kids in.

That magic sparkle.

I wanted to be more than part of her group. I wanted to be her best friend.

To do that, I needed alone time.

That's why, on Wednesday, I joined the newspaper staff.

"Be a joiner," Eden had said.

"You want to write articles?" Roseann beamed at me when I entered Mrs. Murphy's room after school.

"I've never done it, but I thought it would be fun." I sat next to her. "Is it okay that I missed the first meeting?"

"So okay. Mrs. Murphy just explained rules and stuff. And we elected officers." Roseann gestured to the ten kids sitting in the semicircle the desks now formed. "We need more members."

"Where are Grace, Miranda, and the others?" I'd been expecting the group.

"They wanted to do art club. It meets at the same time."

"You don't? Like art, I mean."

"I like art, but I want to be a journalist. Newspaper is a Bleeker thing." She adjusted her stretchy pink headband. Every day her headband or barrette perfectly matched her outfit.

"A Bleeker thing? How's that?" My curls were too wild to tame with a cute headband. I was queen of the messy ponytail.

"The *Hillsbury Herald* has had a Bleeker as the editor for the past five years. Mrs. Murphy expects it. Kate's editor-in-chief this year." She nodded to her sister, who had just walked in with Mrs. Murphy. Kate was a taller version of Roseann, and just as bright and happy. "I'm the sixth-grade editor," Roseann continued.

"Congratulations!"

"Thanks." She scooted her desk closer. "I really want to make our paper great. I want to prove that I can write a great article. Do you too?"

Until ten minutes ago, I hadn't even considered joining the newspaper staff. But now . . . "Sure."

"We should help each other with ideas—"

"That'd be great!" I answered, too fast, but I was excited. "When?"

"I don't know." Roseann waved at a boy across the room. "Hey, Jeremy!"

"Are you and Kate going to the barbeque at the church this weekend?" he asked.

Roseann's attention shifted to him as they made plans to play a game with beanbags and teams they played every year at the barbeque.

Mrs. Murphy clapped her hands, cutting them off. She welcomed the new members and spoke about the upcoming issue.

"Kate will be covering the bus debate for the lead article. Brandon and Elise will do rundowns on the sports teams. What else?" She looked expectantly around the semicircle. "We need feature stories. Stories that will interest the students. Let's throw out ideas."

"Cafeteria food?" the boy next to me suggested.

"What about it?" Mrs. Murphy leaned forwards. "You need an angle. Are you investigating something about the food?"

"Why it's so bad?" he offered.

"That's not a story. How about making up a questionnaire and then write about the students' answers? Think more about it, then come back to us." Mrs. Murphy brushed her wispy bangs out of her eyes. I could see she enjoyed this group. I wondered if she'd ever written for a newspaper.

A girl with cropped hair raised her hand. "I could interview the new teachers. Do a profile on each of them."

Mrs. Murphy looked at Roseann's sister. "What do you think, Kate?"

"That could be good, but it has to be interesting. The teachers won't be all that new by the time the newspaper comes out, so you need to find something special about them. What makes them different from all our other teachers?"

"Exactly!" Mrs. Murphy snapped her fingers. "That's the key. We should highlight special activities and students. Who knows a student who does something incredible?"

"Simon can play chess with his toes," the cafeteria-food boy suggested.

"Big deal," said the girl with cropped hair. "I can play the piano with my toes."

"There's a kid in the eighth grade with webbed toes," another boy offered. "Two of his toes are attached with skin."

"Enough with the toes!" Mrs. Murphy called as everyone giggled. "Let's try for real achievements."

I thought playing piano with toes was a pretty

good achievement. I planned to try that later on Alex's keyboard.

"Tyler Blanchi won the Labor Day running race," another girl said.

"A local race is good," Mrs. Murphy encouraged. "Anything else?"

"I think there's a girl in seventh grade who's competing in a national horse show," Kate said. "Carly something-or-other. She owns her own horse. I heard the horse can jump crazy high."

Everyone liked the idea of tracking down Carly for an interview and taking some action photos of her horse.

I thought about my stepmother, Carmen. She always wore those stretchy beige riding pants and talked about Buddy, her horse.

I wondered if she'd done horse shows. I wondered why I'd never met Buddy. It was weird how Dad had this other life without me.

"Wait!" Roseann called. "I have something that's better than a local or national winner."

"What's better than national?" Kate asked her sister.

"The whole world." Roseann opened her arms wide. "Did you know that we have a student at our school who is training for the Olympics?"

Everyone tried to guess the mystery student, but I'd

stopped listening. I didn't know anyone in this school. I had no chance of coming up with a feature story. My mind was still on Carmen's horse. Dad never wanted Mom to get a dog when they were still married. What was he doing with a horse?

"It's Molly!" Roseann cried.

"What?" I said, hearing my name. "What's me?"

"Molly is an amazing gymnast. She's training to be in the Olympics," Roseann explained to the group. She rested her hand on top of mine.

"That's incredible, Molly." Mrs. Murphy gazed warmly at me, as if seeing me clearly for the first time. No longer was I the girl with the bag of brownie poop. I was Molly Larsen, Olympic hopeful!

"Well, that's not it exactly." I itched to pull my hand out from under Roseann's. "I mean, you never know—"

"It's a hard road to go down." Mrs. Murphy nodded as if she understood and began to turn away.

"I mean, I don't know about *these* Olympics," I began again. Mrs. Murphy's gaze was back on me.

"True, true," Roseann cut in. "It can't be this one coming up. You're too young. But probably the next one. Isn't it fantastic? In four years, Molly Larsen will represent the United States in a competition against the rest of the world!"

"That's so cool!" said cropped-hair girl. "Molly definitely has to be our feature story."

Everyone agreed.

"I don't think . . . you have to know . . ." I took a deep breath. I had to set them all straight. The Olympics were a dream, but so was becoming a movie star or a fashion model. Right now, there was a better chance of me suddenly growing twelve inches and strutting the catwalk in Paris than Andre jumping me to the Elite level. He wouldn't even let me do my back handspring–back tuck yesterday.

"Mrs. Murphy, may I write the article about Molly?" Roseann asked. "We could meet for interviews. Just the two of us." She squeezed my hand.

I squeezed it back. *This* is what I'd wanted. The two of us spending time together. I couldn't mess it up.

"Roseann, are you ready to write such a big feature?" Mrs. Murphy crinkled her forehead. "Maybe it would be best if I gave it to one of the eighth graders."

"No! Please, it's my idea. I really want to do this. Plus, Molly is my friend. We'll work together. A lot."

"I like your passion, Roseann." Mrs. Murphy wrote her name and the assignment on a pad of yellow paper. "I don't usually assign a big feature article to a sixth grader, but Molly's yours. Let's see what you can do."

"I won't let you down." She raised my hand up with hers. "*We* won't let you down."

I wanted to do the right thing. I wanted to tell everyone that I wasn't training to go to the Olympics. I wanted to tell Roseann to write the article about that girl and her horse instead.

It was unreal that they all believed I was *that* good at gymnastics. How had this happened?

Mrs. Murphy ended the meeting, and I still hadn't said anything. I was usually so talkative. Now I couldn't force out the one sentence I needed to say.

"Want to come to my house tomorrow after school?" Roseann asked.

Hanging out one-on-one at her house was huge. After all that time together, I was sure we'd be best friends. *Once that happens,* I reasoned, *I'll tell her it was all a misunderstanding.*

A joke, really.

We'll be such good friends, she'll think it's funny.

We'll laugh about it together. Our little inside joke.

It's fine if Roseann thinks I'm Gold Medal Girl for one more day, I reasoned. I'd stop it tomorrow, before she wrote even the first word of the article.

"Yes," I told her. "I would love to come by your house."

CHAPTER 8

"What happened today?" Eden's face loomed large on my computer screen, ready for the update.

I had five minutes before Mom raced home from work to drive me to the gym. I already wore my red leotard, and my gym bag waited by the garage door. I told Eden about joining the newspaper staff.

"That's what I'm talking about!" Eden exclaimed. "Now you and Roseann have a link. You need to work on a story together."

"We kind of are. I'm going to her house tomorrow."

Eden gave a flurry of little claps. "Hello! You're the best, Molly. You don't invite someone to your house if you don't really like them."

"What about Maddy?" I countered. "You invited her over last spring."

"That was a family thing. Her dad works with my dad. . . ." Eden launched into a long explanation.

I didn't care about Maddy. I was killing time so Eden didn't ask the big question. The topic of our article.

I debated how much to tell her. Eden was as invested in the Roseann Project as I was. She truly wanted me to be happy here and have a great friend. I just wasn't sure if she'd see the whole Olympic thing the way I did. She might see it as lying. Or as bragging. She hated when I boasted about the gymnastic moves I could do that she couldn't.

"What are you guys up to?" I asked to change the subject.

"Sari is having a sleepover party on Friday night." Eden walked across her kitchen to open a cabinet. I knew she was reaching for a glass to pour her favorite iced tea–lemonade mixture. She did that every day after school. "We're going to make it into a spa party. I'm bringing this new aqua nail polish." She wiggled her fingernails at the screen. "Amanda is mixing up the facial mask."

"What's she using?" I tried to hide my hurt. Mixing masks had always been my thing. I was famous for my avocado-honey mask.

"Oatmeal and yogurt."

"That's a good one." My heart ached to be back there. I lined up colored pencils on my desk in my new bedroom. Red, orange, yellow. The order of the rainbow.

Eden told me more about the spa-party plans, and I stared up at my fabric-covered bulletin board. When I'd moved, I'd stripped it of all the clutter. Now it only had two things pinned to it: the photo of me and Eden in matching bathing suits clowning for the camera and a round-trip airline ticket back to Arizona.

"A present for you and Alex," Dad had said that last day, when he took me to the crafts market. He handed us each an envelope.

"Money?" Alex cried.

"Something money can't buy. Well, actually money bought this, but you know, open it. You'll see what I mean," Dad rambled. He sure was having trouble speaking that day. I knew he was sad to see us go so far away.

"It's a ticket," I said as I pulled out a stiff paper from the envelope.

"An airplane ticket. One for each of you," Dad explained. "There's no date on it. You can come see me whenever you want, for as long as you want. You don't need to come together. You call me and say you're coming, and I'll be waiting for you."

"*We'll* be waiting for you," Carmen corrected him. I wished she'd stop trying so hard. She should know, after all our hikes together, that I liked her.

"Exactly." Dad's blue-gray eyes turned moist. "That's what's important. Family. That's what money can't buy."

Alex and I both hugged Dad—and Carmen too.

Now I wondered if I shouldn't use the ticket. I could fly in for the weekend. Go to Sari's spa party. My avocado mask was far superior to any mask made from oatmeal. Avocado softened your skin a whole lot more.

"Daria went on vacation and closed the gym for a week." Eden broke into my thoughts. "All I can do is practice handstands in my room. Boring! You must be working on exciting new stuff. Fill me in."

I glanced at my bedside clock. Mom was late. "Uh, hey, listen, I've got to leave for the gym now. I'll try to text you when I get back, okay?"

"Sure thing." She did our sign-off wave. I did it too.

My stomach began to hurt. Why had I said that? I'd never made an excuse to stop talking to Eden. But I'd never kept this much from her before, either. Not only Roseann and the whole Olympics thing . . . I hadn't told Eden how badly I was doing at Andre's gym! How I was in one of the lowest groups! How Andre had to reteach every move Daria had taught me!

I gazed at my ticket again. I couldn't use it now. It was too soon.

I had to go back victorious.

I could do it too. I just needed some time.

I'd been the star when I'd left. I wasn't going back as anything less.

"Yes, Molly!" Nastia called. "Now you're waking up!"

My palms left chalky prints on my thighs as I leaned over to catch my breath. My head spun from all the handstands I'd done on the uneven parallel bars. I'd never gotten dizzy before. Then again, I'd never done thirty in a row.

I was proud of myself. The energy I'd come into the gym with tonight continued to surge through me. I could change things here. Be a star.

"Over to Andre," Nastia commanded. She directed her attention to the next girl, already turning kip circles.

"Okay!" I skipped across the floor.

"Don't do that." Sofia's hand grabbed my shoulder. "You'll mess up Kelsey."

I stopped, and we watched Kelsey fly through the air in a series of connecting flips and twists. "She's so focused, a charging bull wouldn't bother her," I said.

"Andre wants us to walk as we do in meets. No

running or skipping." Sofia showed me the straight-legged march. I felt like a tin soldier as I followed.

"Quiet your body," Andre said for the fourth time, after I'd already spent an hour with him, trying to perfect the special arabesque. Everyone in my group had long ago moved on to tumbling.

"Move on up . . . move on up . . ." My legs ached to bounce in time with the beat the cheerleaders clapped out over the wall.

I couldn't let the chanting throw off my focus. I locked my knees. I straightened my legs and pointed my toes painfully.

"Tighten up. Stiffen up," Andre barked.

As I held the unnatural position, a popular song blasted from the other side of the wall. Silently I mouthed the words. My hips longed to sway.

"A noodle! You are a noodle!" Andre flung his arms into the air, unable to hide his frustration. "I know you can do this, Moll-le. We are going to work all night until you get it. Then we will work tomorrow. Then the next day."

My stomach twisted in knots. I felt horrible.

"I need to go to the bathroom." My voice didn't sound like my own. Smaller and meeker.

"Fine. Be quick, and then we do it again!" Andre

shooed me off, and I hurried into the empty locker room.

I sat on a bench and pulled my knees into my chest. I didn't have to go to the bathroom. I closed my eyes and let the cheerleaders' chant soothe me. "Keep going . . . keep climbing . . . up, up, up! Keep going . . . keep climbing . . ."

When had gymnastics become so unfun? I wondered.

I thought of calling Mom to come get me. I chipped away at my pink nail polish, wondering if this was a good idea. Before she'd written that huge check to Andre, she'd asked if I was sure about such an intense program. I'd said I was one hundred percent sure. Could she get her money back, if I wasn't so sure anymore?

My body rocked in time with the cheers. I'd been sitting there for a while when I heard the door open.

"Molly? Hey, Molly, Andre's looking for you!" Sofia's raspy voice called into the locker room.

My stomach tightened. I wanted to hide.

"Molly?"

I bolted before I could think. Pulling open the door to the cheering side, I dashed inside. I blinked against the bright lights. Positive slogans painted in primary colors covered the white walls. BE THE BEST YOU! LOUD AND

PROUD! SHOUT IT OUT! Several groups of girls practiced in different areas.

I gazed around, stunned at all the activity. Cheers. Dances. Tumbling.

The locker-room door behind me squeaked open.

I dove behind a pile of mats. My heart thudded as Sofia poked her head in. Could she see me? I tightened my body into a ball.

Sofia looked to the left and right. She shrugged, then returned to the locker room. In a minute or two, she'd tell Andre I was missing. Then what?

Go back, I told myself, but my legs wouldn't follow my brain. I stayed squatted beside the mats and watched the cheerleaders closest to me work on a pyramid. They tried several times to hold the formation. Each time the top girls tumbled onto the thick foam mats. They giggled as they sprawled together, and the coach encouraged them to try again.

Finally they built it all the way up. Girls balanced on shoulders and backs. Total concentration and total trust.

"Ready . . . and . . . ," called a girl from the bottom.

I muffled a gasp as the smallest girl on top launched into a double front tuck. She landed safely in the arms of three girls below.

That's what Shrimp does, I realized. I searched but didn't see her on this side of the gym.

The girls in the pyramid clapped and cheered as they formed a line. Then, at the exact same time, they flew into back handspring–back tucks. Every foot hit the mat at the same moment. Then two girls began a tumbling pass.

This is hard stuff, I thought. I pitched forwards for a better view.

The tumbling flowed into a series of dance moves. Not the ballet-arabesque kind gymnasts do, but party moves. Shimmying, shaking, and twirling. I bobbed my head to the beat.

"Pretty fun, huh?" A tall woman in an orange warm-up jacket that said CHEER COACH gazed down at me.

Busted! In my red leotard, it was clear where I belonged.

"Taking a little break?" she asked. She didn't seem angry.

"Something like that," I mumbled.

She hooked a piece of short blond hair around her ear. "You never know what's behind a door until you open it."

I had no idea what she was talking about, but she wasn't in any hurry to send me back. Side by side, we watched silently as the cheerleaders ran through their routine two more times. At the end, they high-fived each other.

I glanced at the big clock on the wall. Mom would be waiting in the parking lot by now.

"I should go." I headed towards the door.

"Don't be a stranger," the woman called as I slipped unnoticed into the locker room, out through the gymnastics gym, and into Mom's car.

On the ride home, Mom sang to the new Taylor Swift song. I hadn't heard her sing since we moved. I joined in and tried to harmonize on the chorus. Mom covered for me when I messed up, especially on the high notes. She once won a singing competition in her teens.

"I'm getting the hang of this boss thing." She drummed her fingers on the steering wheel. "People told me today that I'm good at what I do."

"That's really great, Mom." She'd already washed off her makeup and put on a gray sweatshirt. She looked so relaxed.

"Alex is making friends. He went to the library tonight for a study group. You found a new gym. It's all coming together." She rolled down the windows and launched into a country song. She belted the chorus loud enough for the driver in the car next to us to turn his head and stare at her while waiting for the red light. She held the high note extralong for him.

I couldn't mess up her good mood. I'd have to deal with the gymnastics thing myself.

CHAPTER 9

"You don't mind walking, do you?" Roseann asked as we left the school together the next afternoon. "My mom drove Jane to buy sneakers. Chrissy has to stay late at the high school."

"Not at all. I walk in the afternoons too, but I go the opposite direction." I pointed down James Street. "Where's Kate?"

"Somewhere around. She walks with her friend Jordana."

I matched my pace with Roseann's. We both wore dark jeans. I'd paired mine with my favorite rose-colored, lace-trimmed tank and a faded denim shirt. I'd put on the turquoise necklace I only wore on special occasions and lots of thin, bangle bracelets. They jangled as I ran my hand along the top of a squared-off hedge.

"Water alert!" Roseann called, and we both dodged the spray from a yard sprinkler.

"You'd get in trouble for that where I used to live," I said.

"For what?" Roseann's blue eyes searched the quiet street.

"Watering your lawn in the middle of the day. In the desert, there's not a lot of water. You can't waste it on making your grass green," I explained. "You can only water at night, when it's cooler. We never had grass in our yard. Just rocks and cactus."

"I'm glad the law isn't the same here, or my family would be locked away for a long time." She pointed to a large green yard that sloped back from the street. Behind a deep red maple tree sat a white clapboard house surrounded by marigolds and other autumn flowers. Two sprinklers were on in full force, wetting the stone pathway leading to the house.

"It's beautiful," I said from the sidewalk.

"Can you believe my dad grew up here too?" Roseann stepped onto the pathway and let out an ear-piercing shriek. Clutching her book bag, she froze. Her lips trembled as she gazed down. Slithering by her navy loafers was a tiny green snake.

"Sn-sn-sna—" Roseann couldn't get the word out.

"Snake," I said. I reached out with my white Converse and nudged the little guy back into the flowers.

"How can you do that?" Roseann stared at me with wonder. "You weren't scared?"

"Of a snake smaller than my foot?" I laughed. "Compared with the snakes back where I lived, that guy looks like an earthworm. You should see the big snakes we have."

Roseann shuddered. "Never. I'm such a scaredy-cat."

The Bleeker house smelled like a mixture of vanilla and jasmine. All the walls were covered in dainty flowered wallpaper. The overstuffed furniture was a mossy sage green. White curtains fluttered at the open windows.

"That's so cool." A vase filled with dozens of red licorice straws sat in the middle of the white wooden kitchen table. Glass jars, the kind that hold cotton balls in bathrooms, were filled with pastel jelly beans and positioned around the house on side tables.

"We're big on candy . . . and salad." Roseann poked her head into the fridge. One shelf was packed with nail polish. "Mom thinks it stays fresher in here," she explained when she saw my questioning look. "Do you like Shirley Temples? Mom mixes them up every afternoon."

Roseann poured us each a glass of bubbly pink

soda and tossed in two maraschino cherries. She peeled back the foil on a mixing bowl in the fridge to reveal chocolate-chip cookie dough. "We could bake cookies."

"We could eat it with spoons," I suggested.

"Even better!" Roseann grabbed two spoons, and we sat at the table. She opened a pink notebook. "Ready to do the interview?"

"We should eat first. I need energy," I said.

We dug our spoons into the raw cookie dough.

"Whoa!" A taller Roseann look-alike with fairer skin swept into the kitchen. "That's mine. I'm making cookies for a bake sale."

"Sorry, Lauren. It's yummy," Roseann apologized to her sister.

"One more spoonful, you goon, and that's all." Lauren grinned.

Roseann and I each took a tiny spoonful, then Lauren pulled the bowl away. Her hair fanned out the same way Roseann's did.

Lauren invited us to help her bake. She pulled out three cute miniscoopers that made the cookies perfectly round.

"I can out-circle you," Lauren challenged.

"Game on!" Roseann cried. "Ready, set, scoop!"

We each tried to make the most circular cookie. I was disqualified because I kept poking my fingers into the dough. Roseann won.

"Your sister's so nice. My brother would've gone nuts if I'd eaten his cookie dough." I told Roseann about the time when Alex discovered that I'd cut his comic books into strips to weave a basket. For revenge, he'd given all my Barbies buzz cuts.

After the cookies had cooled and Lauren left, Roseann tried to get back to the interview. "When did you first start gymnastics?"

I told her all about Daria and her gym. I told her about Eden. I gave a lot of descriptions about learning moves when I was young. I started to relax. *If I can keep the article about this beginning stuff,* I thought, *everything will be all right. Maybe I won't have to fess up at all.*

"Hey, hey, hey!" Kate wandered in and grabbed two licorice straws. She tossed one to me. "Good catch, gymnastics girl."

"Thanks. It's Molly." I'd noticed how Roseann and all her sisters had the same way of holding your gaze when they talked.

"I love your necklace," Kate said. "I have dangly earrings that would match. You should try them later."

"For sure!" One sister was nicer than the next.

Forget being friends, I was ready to move in. A little dark brown hair dye, and I could be the sixth Bleeker sister.

"Are you asking her the hard questions?" Kate peered at Roseann's notes.

"I'm doing background information first," Roseann explained.

"You need to dig deep for a good article." Kate gave her a few pointers as I waited in dread. If I didn't tell soon, Roseann might piece it together herself. What would she do when she found out? Would she make me leave?

"Let's have the article show what it's like to be a top gymnast training for the big time," Roseann said when Kate went upstairs.

"Ew, look, a snake!" I widened my eyes.

Roseann dropped her pen and jumped up. "Where?"

"Gotcha!" I cried.

"Be serious, Molly. I need to do this interview." Roseann picked up her pen. "What does it feel like to do the hardest moves?"

I tried to describe soaring through the air when I do an aerial or back tuck. "For a few seconds, I'm weightless. I'm flying! I get a thrill when I twist in the air and land solidly. I feel fearless."

Roseann scribbled notes as I spoke. I answered questions about our practice routine at the gym. I talked more about Kelsey Wyant and how she trained than I did about myself.

"So you and this girl Kelsey train together?"

"No, not exactly." I hesitated.

"Right, I get it. You're at the same gym, but you're against each other too. Rivals."

"Not rivals. We're not on the same level."

Roseann knocked her head with her pen. "That was silly. You don't have to be modest. I know you're on a higher level. You told me you're at the top."

My mouth felt dry and swallowing suddenly became painful. "Have you ever said something and then wished you hadn't?"

Roseann crossed something off her notes. "Wait. I messed up or I can't read what I wrote. Do you have one coach or two?"

"Two. Andre and Nastia." I tried again. "It's funny how, sometimes, you can be making a joke and no one gets it, you know?"

"What do you mean? Do your coaches have trouble understanding English? Are they from another country?"

"Kind of. I don't know. That wasn't what I was—"

"Can I meet them?" Roseann asked. "Can I come to the gym and get a quote from them for the article? That way it's someone official telling us how amazing you are."

"Andre's not going to say what you think he'll say." I sighed. Time to come clean. "Here's the thing—"

"Do you know what time it is, Roseann?" Another sister with the same silky hair and dark blue eyes as the others walked into the kitchen. By process of elimination, I figured she was Chrissy, the oldest. She wore the cutest short plaid miniskirt, a navy tank top, and sneakers.

"A few more minutes, Chrissy. I was just getting to the good questions. Molly's the new girl I told you about."

"Roseann, there's something funny I need to tell you," I said urgently. "I mean, it's so ridiculous. You'll totally laugh."

"Practice starts in ten minutes in the park. I have to be on time, or they'll fire me as assistant coach." Chrissy grabbed an apple from the refrigerator. Her eyes were highlighted by jet-black mascara that exaggerated the curl of her lashes. "I'm leaving now. You too, Roseann."

"I'm sorry," Roseann said to me as she stood. "I have to go to practice. Can I ask you more questions later?"

"Sure, but . . ." Why couldn't I spit it out?

"Are you coming too?" Chrissy asked me.

"She doesn't play field hockey." Roseann waved away the offer. "She's a gold-medal gymnastics star. Isn't that cool?"

I cringed. It wasn't cool, because it wasn't true. Besides, I didn't want to be only that to Roseann. I wanted to be her friend.

"Yes. I'll come," I announced.

"You will?" Roseann tilted her head.

"If it's okay. I don't know how to play, but I'd like to learn."

"I can teach anyone," Chrissy bragged. "I'm captain of the high school team. We're going all the way to state this year."

"What about gymnastics? Don't you have practice every night?" Roseann asked.

Sitting in Roseann's beautiful house that smelled of freshbaked cookies and flowers and surrounded by her super-nice sisters, one of whom wanted to teach me the sport Roseann and her friends were crazy about, I realized that the last place I wanted to be was the cold and serious gym, where I'd only hear that I looked like a wet noodle again and again.

"No problem. My coach is going to . . . to a meeting

tonight. He said practice was optional." I couldn't believe how easily I'd added another untrue story to the first. "Can I come along?"

"Great! The more the merrier!" Chrissy pumped her fist.

Exactly, I thought. Field hockey was a team sport. If a whole bunch of us moved a ball down a field together, we'd bond and have fun. Gymnastics was an individual sport. I wasn't making friends working on a beam routine by myself.

"Roseann can lend you shorts and a stick," Chrissy said. "Practice runs until six at Dunham Park. If you like it, maybe we can squeeze you onto the team or give you a proper tryout."

I pulled out my phone and texted Alex while Roseann ran to her room.

> no gym 4 me tonite. Going 2 field hockey w/ Roseann & her big sis. pick up @ 6 @ the park???

I held my breath. He had grumbled this morning when Mom told him to drive me to the gym so she could go to a work dinner with the paper-towel client. Would he ask why I wasn't going?

For sure. Play hard, he texted back.

I grinned. So unlike Alex. I wondered what was going on with him.

Roseann returned with an extra pair of mesh shorts and a heavy wooden stick that curved at the end. "This is my old one, but you're shorter than I am. Are you ready?"

"Ready!" I followed Roseann and her sister to the car. Off to practice. Together.

Join in. Share the same interests. Eden would totally agree with my choice to ditch gymnastics for field hockey.

I looked down at the stick. *It can't be too hard to whack a ball with this thing*, I thought. My heart soared. I had a feeling that I'd be good at it.

CHAPTER 10

"Molly? What are you doing here?" Miranda ran over to Roseann and me as we walked onto the field together.

"Trying to learn field hockey." I bowed comically.

"That's awesome!" Miranda laughed and seemed truly glad to see me. So did all the other girls, most of whom I recognized from the lunch table. "It's not too hard."

"I'm thinking: see ball, swing stick"—I gave my stick a wild swing high above my head—"and whack ball into the goal!" I made a roaring-crowd noise.

"Whoa, there, champ!" A muscular woman in a black baseball cap grabbed my wrist and gently lowered it. "Rule one. The stick is never raised higher than your waist. It's dangerous."

"And you'll get a foul," Grace added. Her pale hair was pulled into tight French braids.

"Good to know," I said. "Stick on the ground."

"I'm Coach Nicki. Chrissy told me it's your first time, so welcome to the Eagles." She tilted the visor of her cap to better see me. "You look like you have strong arms and legs. What about those sneakers?"

Grace, Miranda, Roseann, and I stared down at my white Converses. Everyone else wore rubber-soled cleats. "I didn't know I was coming," I explained.

Coach Nicki nodded. "For today, it's okay." She tossed me a pair of long green athletic socks and shin guards. "Pull these on to protect your legs."

"I need protection? Does the stick hurt?" I'd never considered being hit by it.

"Only when it connects with your leg," Coach Nicki said. "Run fast, keep your eyes on the ball, and you'll be fine."

"I have tons of bruises," Miranda confided. She pointed out all her black-and-blues as I pulled on the thick socks.

"Grace is bruise-free, because she runs so fast," Roseann put in.

"You got to keep up with me, Roe. That's how we score." Grace tapped her stick against Roseann's.

Roseann tapped hers back. "You and me. The Dynamic Duo in action."

"They always score the goals," Miranda explained to me.

"Do I look ridiculous?" I wore my rose-colored, lace-trimmed tank with Roseann's baggy black mesh shorts, high green socks, and my new white Converses.

"You look cute," Roseann assured me. She tossed me a pair of goggles. "Put these on too."

"Are we snorkeling?"

"If the ball hits your eye, you can go blind," Miranda put in.

"I see." I slipped the plastic goggles over my head. "Get it? I see?"

Roseann and Miranda groaned at my pun.

"Huddle up!" Coach Nicki called.

The twelve of us gathered around. She introduced me, then we placed our hands into the circle. "Eagles on three. One, two, three—"

"Eagles! Eagles! Eagles!" they all cheered. I joined the group roar, feeling the power of being part of a team.

"Break it out." Coach Nicki divided our group in half. "Stick skills with Chrissy. Running with me."

While Roseann, Grace, Miranda, Anna, and their friend Fiona dribbled the ball in and out of cones, Chrissy had a private session with me.

"Meet Myrtle." She held up her battered stick. "Myrtle is my best friend."

"Your best friend is your field hockey stick?"

"Totally. She's like another body part. Where you go on the field, your stick goes."

"Does everyone name their hockey sticks?"

"The good players do." Chrissy showed me how to grip my stick and use only the flat side.

"What do you think about Stanley Stick? Or Peppermint Stick?" I asked. "How about Captain Hook?"

Chrissy shook her head. "It's a little early for you to be picking out names."

I crouched low and moved the flat side of the stick back and forth to dribble the small, hard ball. My arms twisted like a pretzel.

"Eyes on the ball!" Coach Nicki walked over.

"I'm watching it. I watch it go over here. I watch it go over there," I joked.

"Make it go straight," Coach Nicki instructed.

"This ball has a mind of its own," I told Chrissy.

"It's a special trick ball we give first timers," she whispered.

"Seriously?" That would explain a lot.

"Not seriously." Chrissy fixed my grip. "You're in good athletic shape. No huffing or puffing, but you need to get the feel of the stick. Remember, it's your friend."

I tried again. One ball shot to the far left. The next ball flew off to the right. "My friend doesn't like me."

"Try a flick," Chrissy suggested.

Roseann and Grace stopped dribbling to watch me. My stomach fluttered. I didn't want to mess up again.

"Flip? Did you say a flip?" I called out. Then I dropped my stick and did three back handsprings, landing next to one of my many off-course balls. "Ta-da! A flip!" I cried.

Roseann and Grace clapped.

"Enough funny business," Coach Nicki said. I tried not to blush. I just thought I'd crack a joke.

Chrissy lined us up for offense-defense drills.

"Ow!" My partner, Miranda, cringed after my stick whacked my own shins for the fifth time. "Molly, you can't stand in one place like that. You need to keep moving."

"No pain, no gain," I joked. My legs throbbed. I'd be black and blue tomorrow. "I'm too busy trying to slap the ball to move my body."

"You've got to do both!" Grace called. She and Roseann performed the drill perfectly next to us.

"Scrimmage time!" Coach Nicki called after I'd messed up the drill several more times.

"What about me?" I asked.

"You're far from ready, but get on the field and see what you can learn. Stay out of the action and over by the sidelines. Try to pick up on what the others are doing," she suggested.

I watched Roseann high-five Grace even though they were on opposite scrimmage teams. I longed to be the other half of Roseann's Dynamic Duo.

Forget staying on the sidelines, I decided. I was going to play—and play hard.

Fifteen minutes later, I was sweating. Not from the running. Jump roping and conditioning had me in good shape. I sweated from trying to get my stick on the ball. These girls were like magicians. The ball would be clearly in front of me. I'd swing my stick back, readying to hit it, and *wham*! Someone would magically scoop the ball out of my path. Some girls shouldered me away. Hard! Twice, I tripped over my own feet and face-planted on the grass.

"You okay, Molly?" Roseann called from across the field. How could she talk to me while blocking a shot and stealing the ball away from Anna? I couldn't even stop hitting myself in the shins with my own stick!

"Perfect," I called back. I stopped running and stood, watching the action.

I hated this game, I decided. I hated the tiny ball. And I hated my nameless hooked stick. We were never going to be friends.

Just as I was about to tell Coach Nicki I was done, I heard Roseann call. "Molly! It's coming to you!"

The ball rolled right in front of me. No one blocked me. Why would they?

This is it, I realized. My chance to shine.

I lined up my stick and began to move the ball forwards.

"Go, Molly!" I heard Chrissy yell.

"Molly! Molly!" Roseann cried.

The goal stood in the distance, and Grace, in her yellow scrimmage pinny, stood in between, ready to block. *I'm getting by her,* I promised myself. *I can do this!*

My legs, arms, and stick began to work together. Faster and faster, I moved the ball upfield. I spotted Miranda in a yellow pinny off to my right side, so I darted left.

"Molly!" Roseann cried.

I was on fire! I heard Roseann cheering, and that pushed me even faster.

Grace was upon me now. She stood a head taller than me. *No way is she stopping me,* I thought. *No way!*

I faked left, but she moved with me. *Time to show*

Roseann what I can do, I thought, eyeing the goal nervously. Barreling past wasn't an option, so I got creative. Tapping the ball to the right, I sprang into a split leap, startling Grace. She gaped at me as I sailed past her in the air. I landed by the ball and took it up towards the goal.

Ha! I bet she'd never seen a player do a gymnastics leap before.

Footsteps pounded on the field behind me. My name was called over and over. I felt the power of my team as they surrounded me. I charged forwards. Roseann ran up my right side, ready to help. The new Dynamic Duo. Time to score!

With a burst of energy, I sped towards the goal. I pulled my stick back wide. *Power,* I thought. *Power it in!*

I had to make this shot.

Fiona ran in to defend their goal. Her dark eyes widened as I gave my most awesome swing. I heard my stick connect. The ball soared powerfully through the air . . . and far from the goal. My stick kept moving, and I lost my grip.

I watched in horror as my heavy wooden stick spiraled sideways into the sky—right for Roseann's head!

CHAPTER 11

I screamed and screamed as the stick boomeranged straight for Roseann.

Grace leaped into action. She dove and flung her arms around Roseann's waist, pulling them both to the ground.

The stick whizzed by. My screams echoed throughout the park.

We all raced to where the two girls lay panting.

"I'm sorry. I'm so, so sorry," I repeated. I felt awful.

"I'm fine." Roseann sounded shaken, but she wasn't hurt.

"Grace, you saved Roseann from being beheaded by Molly's stick!" Miranda patted Grace on the back. Everyone cheered for Grace. Roseann hugged her.

"Never, and I mean *never*, do you raise your stick above your waist!" Coach Nicki scolded me. Her face was red.

"I'm sorry," I said. "I got carried away. And then, I guess, my stick got carried away too."

No one laughed at my lame joke. Especially not Roseann. The girls gathered around her as if she'd just survived a plane crash. I gazed where the stick had landed, several feet away. By my guess, it would have missed her even if Grace hadn't tackled her to the ground.

I decided to keep this calculation to myself.

Coach Nicki pulled me aside. "I'm thinking you may not be ready for the team just yet. We should have you join a clinic or take a few lessons."

"I could do that," I agreed. "Then maybe later I could be on the team."

"No! You have gymnastics. You can't give that up." Roseann came up behind us. The rest of the team trailed her.

"No offense, Molly, but I'm not sure field hockey is your thing," Grace added.

"She *is* supergood at gymnastics," Miranda told Coach Nicki.

"I got that sense on the field." Coach Nicki winked at me. "It's great to do a sport that you love."

Did I love gymnastics? I knew I didn't love field hockey. I wanted to be on a team with Roseann, but this might not be the best way to go.

"Give your pinnies to Chrissy," Coach Nicki instructed. "Good practice, girls. See you all next week."

Not me, I thought. I listened as Grace and Roseann recounted Grace's heroic save. Joining field hockey hadn't gone as I'd planned. It certainly hadn't brought Roseann and me closer. But I guess that's what happens when you nearly take off someone's head.

Trudging to the sidelines, I spotted my brother standing alongside Chrissy. He smirked at me, and I knew he'd seen it all. Boy, would Alex tease me tonight!

Great. Just what I needed.

Alex didn't stay home long enough to tease me. He dropped me off, then disappeared.

"What's with the mystery?" I asked Mom later in our backyard. "Why wouldn't he tell me where he's going?"

Mom hunched over and pulled a hoe through a big section of dead grass. "He went to the library to help a friend study."

"What friend? Who's his friend?" I demanded. How was my shy brother making all these friends already?

"I don't know, honey." She grunted as she dug out the weeds. "I wished he'd stayed and helped. I wanted to lay the seed tonight too."

"I can help," I offered. Mom hadn't noticed that I was home earlier than I'd normally be if I were at the gym. She was too focused on pulling up our backyard and planting grass seed. She said she'd always dreamed of a lush, green yard filled with flowers and walkways.

"Once our yard blooms, this house will feel cozier and settled," she explained.

I knelt beside her and used my hands to yank out the stubborn weeds.

"We could plant a vegetable garden in that corner." Mom pointed towards the fence.

"That would be fun, but don't you need to know how?" I looked around our yard. The old grass had been mostly pulled up, leaving behind a field of tan dirt. "Do you have any idea how to turn all this dirt to food?"

"We'll figure it out together. All three of us. The Larsen farmers!" She hacked with the hoe. "Alex promised to help with the yard this month for gas money."

"Good luck with that," I quipped. "He's never around anymore."

Mom regarded me. "I didn't think you'd care. You two bicker so much when you're together."

I shrugged. "It's not so bad. It's just what we do." The house felt quiet without him.

"You know, I could track down that woman at work and get her daughter's phone number for you. Sheila, I think her name is. You could text her."

Sheila. I imagined a girl my age in the tailored dresses Mom wears to work. A mini-businesswoman with heels and her hair pulled into a bun. She and I would not get along.

"I don't need it, Mom. I'm making great friends already." Even if things weren't going totally smoothly with Roseann, I wasn't going to blow it! She and I had bonded this afternoon at her house. I told Mom about Roseann and her sisters. She was happy for me.

After Mom had gone upstairs to take a shower, I sat at the patio table with my computer to video chat with Eden. I told her everything, minus the bit about the Olympics. When I gave a play-by-play of the flying stick, Eden doubled over with laughter. I joined in with my hiccup laugh.

"Funnicst story ever," Eden said.

"Roseann didn't think so."

"She was just surprised. Of course she thinks it's funny," Eden said. "Tell me more about her house." Eden was fascinated with all things Bleeker. From all the way across the country, she'd caught the Bleeker bug, just like every kid in my new town.

"I can't wait to meet her," Eden said after we reviewed the entire afternoon. "I'm begging my mom to let me visit you as a Christmas gift."

"Yoo-hoo! Hey, Molly!" Shrimp bellowed from somewhere behind the fence.

"What's that?" Eden asked.

"Shrimp's calling. Remember the tiny girl on the trampoline that I told you about?" I stood. "Hey, Shrimp!" I yelled.

"Is she friends with Roseann?" Eden asked.

"I don't think they're close, but Roseann is friends with everyone. Besides, Shrimp kind of does her own thing. I'm going to go see what she wants. Talk later, okay?"

"Okay, but remember the next part of the plan. Be happy. Be the nicest girl on the planet. Go out and get Roseann."

"Got it, Dr. Eden!" I logged off and hurried to the corner of the fence. "Shrimp! You there?"

"Yep, just practicing your favorite game," Shrimp replied.

"What's that?"

"Hmmmm . . . limbo? Pole vaulting? I know it's

something"—Shrimp chuckled—"with a flying stick."

"Oh, no!" I groaned. "You heard about that already?"

"It's awesome! Did you even score?"

"Not even close," I admitted.

"And I thought *I* was the worst at team sports! Want to do flips on my trampoline with me?"

"Yes!" I cried, relieved that Shrimp didn't find the field hockey mess up a big deal. Hopefully Roseann felt the same. "How do I get to you?"

"I live on Royal Oak Drive. You have to go down your street, across Maple, and then down my street," Shrimp told me through the fence.

"My mom's in the shower. She won't let me walk around the new neighborhood by myself yet. I guess I'm stuck here tonight. If only this fence wasn't so high . . ."

"Could you climb it?"

"If I had a ladder or a rope," I said.

"I have an idea. Wait there!" I heard Shrimp run off.

Five minutes later, she returned. She made a few grunting sounds.

"What's going on?" I hated not being able to see.

"Almost done," Shrimp said. "I need to make sure these knots are tight."

"What knots? What are you doing?"

"Catch this!" Shrimp called.

A huge piece of pale pink fabric sailed over the high fence. I grabbed the end and pulled it towards me. The fabric kept coming and coming. Pink, then beige, then yellow, then white, like an enormous never-ending magician's scarf. "What is this thing?"

"I tied a few bedsheets together. Pretty smart, huh? You can use it as a ladder. I tied some extra knots along the way."

"It's genius!" I gave it a tug.

"My end is tied to a tree. Can you shimmy up? If you don't want to, I can climb to you."

"Oh, I'm coming! I'm not scared. Ready?"

"Ready, spaghetti! I'm holding on too," Shrimp called.

I scaled the sheet ladder the same way we had to climb the ropes in gym class. Holding on to the sheets tightly with my hands, I wrapped my feet around the bottom. I used my arm strength and the knots to pull myself up. The sheet ladder swayed as I inched my way up. Twisting around at the top, I shimmied down Shrimp's side of the fence.

Shrimp cheered when I landed. Her yard was the same size as mine, but with lots of flower beds and shrubs. Together we scrambled onto her big, round trampoline. At first we just bounced. Then we competed to see who jumped the highest. Shrimp could really fly!

"Try this," she said. She did a front somersault into a half twist.

"Wow! You're good." I completed it on the third try.

We did front and back tucks. We timed them together, jumping as a pair. We even made up a routine.

"I looked for you in the gym today," Shrimp said as we flipped. "You ditched for field hockey, I guess."

"Big mistake!" I did a split jump.

"Try it touching your toes." Shrimp split her legs and stretched her fingers to her toes.

"Anyway, Andre was probably happy to have a break from me," I said. "I kind of needed a break too."

"Gymnastics isn't good?" Shrimp asked.

"It's not what I thought it would be." I touched my toes in the split jump.

"What did you think it would be?"

I thought it would be fun, like in my old gym in Arizona. I thought my teammates would encourage me, like my old teammates did. I thought the coach would praise me, like Daria did. I thought I'd be good enough to train for the Olympics and then I wouldn't have to feel as if I misled Roseann.

I didn't say any of this out loud. Instead I answered,

"I just thought it would be different."

"You have two choices." Shrimp did a front tuck. "You can quit."

"I'm not a quitter," I said forcefully.

"I didn't mean that." Shrimp stopped jumping. "Or, choice two—our cheer coach says when something is hard, you just have to work harder."

"That's what I'm going to do. Work harder." The sky darkened as the sun set. "What's that noise?"

"I don't hear anything." We sat back-to-back on the trampoline and listened, quiet, catching our breaths.

"All that chirping and trilling," I said. "It's so loud.'

"The crickets? Or the tree frogs?"

"No idea. Night never sounded like this at home."

"I don't even hear it. We moved to Hillsbury when I was four."

"Four was probably easier than twelve." I rested my head on my knees.

"Probably," Shrimp agreed. "I remember being scared of the grass. Isn't that crazy? We came from New York City. I hated how the grass felt all prickly on my bare feet."

"My mom really wants grass. She's trying to grow it in our backyard."

"Can't be that hard. Look around. Everyone has it."

Shrimp waved her arms at her own yard, covered in shadows as dusk fell.

"Lots of times at night, we'd hear coyotes howling," I told her.

"Really? C.J. would freak out. He'd be hiding in my parents' bed. No, *under* it!" Shrimp rubbed her palms together. "I'm *so* going to howl at his bedroom door tonight."

"That's not nice," I scolded.

"True. But it's funny, and he really does like it. It's what we do, you know?"

I thought about me and my brother. "Yeah," I told her. "I do know."

The crickets chirped ever louder in the trees. "I need to climb back over the fence before my mom finds out where I went," I said.

"I need to return the sheets to the closet before my mom finds out what I did," Shrimp agreed.

I jumped off the trampoline. Shrimp found a stepladder in her garage. We flung the knotted sheets back over the fence. With the ladder and the sheets, I was able to twist over the top and slide back into my yard.

"Bye-bye, french fry!" Shrimp called into the darkness.

"Good night, Shrimp."

Later, as I lay in bed listening to the crickets, I thought about Roseann. When Eden and I had planned out being friends with the It Girl, it'd seemed easy. A big smile. A few jokes. Instant friendship.

But in real life, it was not so easy. Not really.

I thought about Shrimp's coach's words: *The harder it is, the harder you have to work.*

The next week, I worked hard at being happy, just as Eden suggested. Her mother had written on her blog that happy people are attracted to other happy people. She said friendliness goes a long way. I planned to out friendly Roseann. Or, at least, be equally as friendly.

When Roseann said she liked my periwinkle nail polish, I loaned her the bottle. I complimented her on her oral report in social studies, because she really did do a great job. I cheered extraloudly for Miranda during the fifty-yard dash in gym. I offered to throw away Grace's trash at lunch when I stood to dump mine. I went back to the gym. I worked on my beam moves with Nastia without complaining.

No one talked about the field hockey stick near miss.

Everyone stopped calling me Ugga Bugga except Lyla, not that I cared about her.

But the strangest thing was that Roseann didn't mention the article. Could she have forgotten about it? I wondered. Did she decide to write something else?

"Um, what's going on with the article?" I whispered on Wednesday morning, leaning towards her desk in social studies.

"Kate said I should write a draft with the information you gave me, then interview you again to fill in the holes," she whispered back. "I'm still writing. I think it's good, though. Mrs. Murphy's going to be impressed."

I couldn't let her do all that work and then drop the bomb that I wasn't going to the Olympics.

Even though I was trying hard, I didn't think that I'd *ever* be going. Unless it was as a spectator.

"I have to talk to you," I said.

"Quiet, girls," Mrs. Murphy called. "Filling in your Europe map is an individual assignment."

I hurried to lunch early that day, hoping to catch Roseann. Shrimp waved, but I was too nervous to go over. I rehearsed three different ways to tell Roseann that my Olympic dreams had all been a joke. Nothing sounded good.

I have to do this fast, I decided. *Rip off the bandage as soon as she walks in.*

Roseann arrived with Ms. Fairley, the Earth Science teacher with the cat's-eye glasses, and a tall boy I didn't know. They talked about a car wash for hurricane victims. I waited impatiently. By the time she finished and had greeted a bunch of other kids, our table had filled up.

Roseann bit into her sandwich, and I peeled back the foil from my strawberry yogurt. I didn't need an audience. I'd have to find Roseann alone later.

"We need to win," Grace announced over the roar of the lunchroom. "We need to finish the dance."

"There's a winner for each grade, right, Roseann?" Miranda asked.

I poked my plastic spoon into the yogurt and leaned forwards to hear better.

"Yes. Kate won in sixth grade, but she didn't win last year. Her eighth-grade group has been practicing *a lot*. They're singing a song with three-part harmony," Roseann reported.

"We can sing too." Fiona straightened her blue-framed glasses.

"Not me. I look horrible when I sing," Miranda confided. "We should stick to dancing, so we can look pretty."

"Look pretty for what?" I finally asked.

"The fall talent show is Friday, in front of the whole school. It's a big deal," Roseann explained.

"We want to win," Grace put in.

"Competitive much?" Miranda teased.

Grace wanted to win at everything. I'd figured that out already.

"We had a big sleepover this summer and choreographed a dance. Well, most of it. We need to practice," Roseann explained.

"That sounds cool," I said, twirling my spoon into the pink yogurt.

"We don't have much time," she added, "especially since we have to fix it up for the six of us."

I quickly added up Roseann, Grace, Miranda, Anna, and Fiona. They made five. Was I number six?

"We need cool matching outfits," Grace said. "Really grown-up and sophisticated."

"I agree. Nothing cute or babyish," Fiona added. "No tutus like we talked about."

"How about stretchy black miniskirts?" Anna suggested. "Does everyone have one of those?"

"Molly, do you have one?" Roseann asked when I didn't chime in.

My heart gave a thump. "I'm in the group?" I asked.

"Obviously!" Roseann gave me a playful nudge. "You need to look really good for the camera too."

"What camera?"

"A professional photographer comes to the school and photographs each group. The photos are put up in the main hallway for parents' night. It's called the Hall of Fame. The winner's photo is put in a gold frame," Roseann explained, "and it stays there for the whole year."

"We so need to look extragood, because we're going to be in that winning photo," Grace said. "What should we wear on top?"

The girls continued speaking, but I barely heard them.

I'd done it!

I was friends with Roseann Bleeker.

I was friends with Roseann Bleeker's friends!

They didn't have to discuss whether or not to include me in the talent show group. They assumed I'd be in it with them. I *belonged*!

"Molly, are you good with a silky, sleeveless top too?" Anna asked. She was the most into fashion of the group. She ripped pages out of magazines and carried them to school to show us her favorite outfits.

"We're doing jewel tones," Grace added. "Turquoise, ruby red, royal blue, jade green."

"I don't have that," I admitted. The tops I owned were mainly T-shirts, spaghetti-strap tanks, and sweaters. Nothing silky.

"You can borrow one from me. Lauren has a silky red one that would look great on you," Roseann offered.

Roseann and I were now sharing clothes! And she trusted me with her big sister's top. Eden was going to flip.

"You're the best," I told Roseann, and I meant it.

"What about the dance? We should get together to teach it to Molly," Miranda suggested. "I kind of forgot some of it too."

"Seriously, Miranda?" Grace wrinkled her nose.

"Well, we never really finished it," Roseann reminded her. "We need to add more steps."

"Come to my house tomorrow after school!" I blurted out.

I could see it now. Roseann and all the other girls dancing in my family room. The six of us together onstage and the crowd going wild. The photo of us in our silky tops hanging in the winning gold frame in the school hall. Roseann and me standing arm in arm in the middle. Best friends.

Every kid walking by the photo would point out Roseann and Molly Larsen, the new girl. They wouldn't be able to put a name to it, but they'd all recognize that we shared the It Girl sparkle.

Me and Roseann.

Best friends forever!

CHAPTER 12

I flung my book bag to its usual spot on the hall floor as I raced into my house Thursday after school. Roseann and crowd would be here soon. My fingers tingled as I thought of it. We were going to have so much fun.

I eyed the bag again, then scooped it up and tossed it into the hall closet. Alex's dirty sneakers lay farther down the hall. I tossed those into the closet too. I added yesterday's newspaper and a sweater draped over a chair. The house had to look good.

I opened the sliding door from the family room to the patio. It was a beautiful day. I wondered if we should have our snack out here.

I hurried into the kitchen. Breakfast dishes still lay on the table. Alex was supposed to clear. Never going to happen, I realized. I plopped them into the dishwasher without scraping them. Opening the cabinet, I found a big bag of sour gummy worms. I remembered Roseann's jelly bean jars. I searched for jars, but we had none. I settled on the tiny glasses we used for juice. I filled each with candy and placed them around the house.

Then I pulled out the box of cupcakes Mom had bought last night. When I told her about the girls coming over, she was so excited for me. She offered to bake her famous double-chocolate brownies.

"No way!" I cried. I couldn't risk reminding them of the brownie-poop mess.

Instead she agreed to drive to the cupcake store. They had a big banner outside, proclaiming they'd won a cupcake competition on TV. I chose seven prize-winning cupcakes, all different flavors. All super-pretty.

Now I placed them on a big plate. Then I raced about, fluffing the sofa pillows and spraying the rooms with Mom's perfume. I paused outside Alex's closed bedroom door, listening to the ping of a video game from his computer. He was supposed to be in charge of me after school, but it wasn't as if I needed a babysitter. I crossed my toes that he'd stay hidden.

In my room, I pulled on my stretchy black skirt and examined myself in the mirror. It was a little tight. Last year, Eden and I had bought black skirts, tights, and tanks for Halloween. We'd been vampire cats, complete with bloody plastic fangs and ears. I even carried a stuffed animal mouse.

I left on my T-shirt. Roseann was bringing me her silky top. Our one rehearsal was a dress rehearsal because the talent show was tomorrow. I wondered what shoes everyone was wearing. Roseann and Grace kept talking about looking grown-up and cool. Would we wear makeup to school? All I owned was lip gloss. Maybe I could borrow some of Mom's.

I rushed back downstairs, grabbed a plaid tablecloth, then hurried out to the patio. I tried to make the metal table look festive. I wished we had flowers. I'd cut them and put them in a vase or jug. I looked around the yard. All we had was dirt and the grass seed Mom had planted last weekend.

And Shrimp flying through the sky.

I watched her twist and twirl. Up, then out of sight again.

"What's the deal, banana peel?" she called to me.

"Hey!" I called back. I tiptoed over to the fence. I wasn't supposed to walk on the grass seed. Mom warned that stepping on it would stop it from sprouting. I heard Shrimp scramble down from her trampoline to our special spot. We'd found a place in the fence where two boards had warped enough that we could peek with one eye through to the other side.

"Whatcha doing?" she asked.

"Roseann and Grace and Miranda and them are coming over to practice our dance for the talent show. Do you know about that?"

"Sure do. I'm doing a tumbling thing."

"With who?" I asked.

"With me. It's going to be awesome. I'm going to use that new song from Two Hearts. The one with that crazy techno beat."

"That's a great tumbling song," I agreed.

Shrimp sure was brave to get up in front of the whole grade by herself. "Did you work out a routine?"

"Nah. I'll play the music and do what feels right. It's more fun to just let loose," Shrimp said. "What kind of dance are you doing?"

"I have no idea," I admitted. "They're going to show me today."

"Good luck. Hey, here's a move. Can you see me?"

"Yeah." I peered through the gap. Shrimp wore her black Lycra shorts, a neon-green tank, and her white cheering sneakers. She stood in a straddle, circled her upper body as she leaned back. Then she popped up and flung her head back and forth as she swayed her hips. "Whaddya think? New dance move from cheer."

"Wild! Can you teach me?"

"Later, for sure. I'm off to cheer practice."

"I have gymnastics tonight. Maybe I'll see you in the locker room." Knowing silly Shrimp was dancing on the other side of the Top Flight wall gave me a good feeling.

"Mañana, iguana!" Shrimp called.

I wondered if she'd ever run out of funny sayings. I hoped not.

Back inside, I glanced at the clock. Everyone would be here in a few minutes. I decided to make lemonade from the powdered mix we had. I raced into the kitchen.

"Are you kidding me?" I cried when I saw what Alex had done.

Buttercream icing dotted the corners of his mouth. He held a chunk of red velvet cake in his hand. On the plate, the crumpled wrappers from four other cupcakes lay in a pile of crumbs alongside smears of icing.

"I'm loving this one. Don't buy that chocolate one again, and the lemon was too tart." Alex licked his lips. "I saved this vanilla-looking one for you. You like vanilla, right?"

"I can't believe you!" I screamed. "You ate all my cupcakes!"

"Not all. I saved two for you. And the rest of this red

velvet guy." He held out his hand. "You don't own all the food in this house."

"Mom bought those for me. Me! Not you. Don't you listen? I told you at dinner last night that my friends were coming over!"

"Oops. My bad." Alex shrugged.

"What am I supposed to do now?" I demanded.

"Cut these last two into pieces. Mini cupcakes. Make a new thing." Alex smirked, totally not understanding how serious this was.

"No one wants cut-up cupcakes that you put your gross fingers in." I grabbed the plate from him and dumped the rest in the garbage.

"Sorry, Mollster," Alex said sheepishly.

"Yeah, great." I pulled Mom's chore list off the refrigerator door. "You might want to finish some of these before I tell Mom what you did, 'cause I'm going to tell."

"You can't!" he protested.

"Watch me."

Alex swiped the list from my hand, grumbling as he disappeared into the garage.

Now what? We had no cookies or chips in the pantry. Last week Mom had announced that she was eating too much junk from the vending machine in her office, so she didn't want to be tempted at home.

I'd give anything to get my hands on that vending machine right now, I thought. With all the coins in my piggy bank, I'd buy great snacks.

I stared into the open refrigerator. *Okay,* I told myself. *This is like that cooking show on TV.* The one where they give the contestants weird ingredients that don't go together, and they have only a few minutes to create a fabulous meal.

Ready, set, go!

I pulled out a bag of baby carrots, a tub of cream cheese, and two green apples. From the pantry, I snagged a jar of Nutella, Ritz crackers, honey, and shelled sunflower seeds. Lining up all my ingredients on the counter, I jumped into action.

I laid out the crackers on a big plate. On some I spread Nutella and cream cheese. On others I spread cream cheese and honey. They looked like something you'd serve at a doll's tea party. I wondered about combining honey and Nutella, then decided against it. Instead, I sliced the apples and smeared them with honey. Then I sprinkled sunflower seeds on top. The carrots I just dumped into a bowl.

Not bad, I thought as I placed the plates on the patio table. If I was on the TV show, I'd make it to the next round.

A few minutes later, they all arrived, and I changed into the silky red shirt Roseann handed me. The fabric smelled of vanilla and jasmine, just like her house. The shirt belonged to Lauren. I promised to take extragood care of it. Roseann wore a matching silk shirt in jade green.

I watched her quietly leave a pink notebook and pen on our front hall bench. I wanted to believe she planned to take notes for the talent show, but I knew better. That notebook was for me—for the follow-up questions to her article. I pretended I hadn't seen it.

"Where's your grass?" Miranda asked, as I brought everyone onto the patio.

For a moment, we all stopped and stared at the expanse of brown dirt that now made up the yard. Mom had raked it flat after laying down the seed. The dirt looked dusty and dry, which meant that Alex had forgotten to water it.

"We're growing it. Starting fresh," I explained brightly. "Who's hungry? I have snacks."

Roseann examined the crackers and the apple slices. Grace scrunched up her face. Fiona scrunched up her face too. No one reached for anything.

"How about a taste test?" I tried. "See what combo works best?" I explained the choices.

Everyone tried a cracker. They weren't terrible, but no one wanted a second. The sticky seed-covered apples lay untouched. My snacks were weird. I could see that now.

"How about a blindfold test? They'll taste better if you can't see them." I laughed, just as Dad had taught me.

"How about we eat later, Molly?" Roseann said. "We should work on the dance."

I sighed. Roseann hadn't said anything mean, but she hadn't laughed along with me, either. Just like with the brownie mess.

"Wait here." I ran back into the house and gathered all the juice glasses of sour gummy worms. I handed them out when I returned.

"Much better," Roseann agreed, sucking the sugar off a green worm.

We lined up on the patio and began to piece together moves. Roseann hooked up her iPod to portable speakers and blasted a Beyoncé song they'd selected. She showed me the steps they'd worked out.

As I followed along, Alex wandered onto the patio. He glanced at the leftover snacks, then kept moving towards the side of the yard. *They must really be bad if my brother, the human vacuum, won't eat them,* I realized.

Then again, he had just demolished five of my gourmet cupcakes.

I raised my arms and twirled slowly with the group.

What was Alex doing? I squinted into the sun. Mom's chore list peeked out of his back pocket. He knelt along the side of the yard with a bag of . . . were they onions?

Who planted onions? And why now, when my new friends were here?

I wanted to yell at him to get away. But then I thought of how Roseann and her sisters seemed to be the best of friends. I sensed her watching him too. If I said anything, I'd look mean. I didn't want to look mean. I kept dancing. Finally Alex strolled around the side of the house towards the garage, out of sight.

"Miranda, stop elbowing me!" Grace cried.

"I need more space," Miranda complained. She was the tallest, and her arms and legs were long and lanky.

"Just don't flail so much," Grace said. "Let's try again. Ready, and . . ."

"Whoa, Miranda. Now you're in my space!" Anna said.

"Your space?" Miranda pushed her bangs from her eyes.

"Yeah. This area"—Anna waved her arms to her

sides and in front of her—"is my space. I can't dance if you invade my space."

"We need more room," Roseann decided. "Everyone off the patio. Hey, Molly, is it okay if we dance out here?"

Mom had instructed me not to step on the grass seed. I chewed my lip, wondering what would happen if the seeds were pushed deeper into the earth. I didn't think it would be that bad. We weren't going to be out here that long. "Sure, just dance lightly."

"This is much better," Roseann said after we'd spread out. "Grace, Fiona, Anna, and I will stand up here. Molly and Miranda stand behind us."

"You're trying to hide me, aren't you?" Miranda seemed amused, not upset.

"No offense, Flick, but you're a little klutzy," Roseann replied.

"A little? I'd say a lot!" Miranda giggled.

Why was I being stuck in the back? I wasn't klutzy. I was a good dancer.

Don't ask, I warned myself. *You're part of Roseann's group. Don't get greedy.*

I stood beside Miranda and dodged her windmill arms.

"I'm copying everything you do," Miranda told me.

"Sure thing!" I said.

We all practiced the dance Roseann and Grace had made up. The movements were jerky and stiff and seemed more like poses to me.

"Yoo-hoo, Molly? Are you paying attention?" Grace called. "We're changing the arm movement to up-and-down."

"Got it." I followed along, feeling as if I were doing jumping jacks instead of dancing. . . .

"Hold up!" I said finally.

Fiona turned off the music.

"Don't take this the wrong way, but the steps don't go with the music. The beat's much faster." I clapped out the rhythm. "We need to move our bodies more like this." I did a full-body shimmy.

Fiona started up the music, and I let my body groove to the beat. I shook my hips and shoulders. I loosened up the moves and added a few of my own. I flung my hair and rolled my neck. The steps came naturally to me. I windmilled my arms like Miranda, then touched the ground.

"What do you think?" I asked when I finished.

Roseann shook her head. "You're a great dancer, Molly, but we're going to look silly if we do that."

"No, we won't," I promised. "We need to add more pop. More wow!"

"I liked the dance moves they way we had them," Grace protested.

"Me too," Fiona agreed. I'd begun to notice she agreed with everything Grace said or did.

"Molly's way looks fun," Miranda spoke up.

"If we do it Molly's way, we're going to be all messy and sweaty," Roseann said. "I thought we all decided we wanted to look pretty. Kind of like models."

"We do," Grace agreed. "Our moves are very sleek. We just need to fix the timing, so we do them at the same exact moment."

I didn't agree. The moves might be sleek, but they were boring. We were dancing to a fun, upbeat song, yet we were barely moving.

Then I remembered all of Eden's advice. *Be happy. Be a joiner.* I sounded like a downer. I shut my mouth and did the moves the way Roseann wanted them.

"Molly!" Alex stuck his head out his second-story bedroom window a while later.

"What?" I called back, apologizing to everyone for stopping in the middle.

"I'm driving you to gymnastics in fifteen minutes!"

"We're not finished," Anna said to me.

"I'm not going today!" I yelled up to Alex.

"Oh, yes, you are! Mom left me in charge, and I'm doing everything on this list. That includes driving you to gymnastics!"

I groaned. I really must've scared him earlier.

"I won't tell Mom about the cupcakes!" I called. "I promise."

"No deal. I planted daffodil bulbs, and I organized the tools in the garage. I'm doing it all, because I need the car tonight to go to the library. Be ready!" He slammed the window shut.

"Ignore him," I said to the others. "Let's practice."

"But don't you have to go to the gym?" Roseann asked. "We don't want to mess up your training."

"You're not messing me up." My stomach twisted. I wished I'd told her the truth days ago. If all the others weren't here, I'd do it right now. "I can be a little late to finish the dance with you. This is important."

"If you're sure . . ." Roseann sounded worried.

"I'm sure." I turned the music back on and took my place next to Miranda.

As we hit the third twirl, a burst of water shot up. Automatically I lifted my head, searching the blue sky for rain. It took a moment to register that water was spraying *up* at me from the ground. And not from one spot. A second and third geyser started up.

"Help!" Roseann squealed as a stream hit her on her neck.

"What's happening?" Fiona cried. Water splattered her blue-framed glasses.

"Molly?" Miranda screamed, dodging the rotating spray.

"The sprinklers!" I yelled. What were the in-ground sprinklers doing on?

More sprinklers popped up from the ground. Cold water blasted at hurricane force from everywhere at once. My clothes stuck to my body, and wet hair flopped in my eyes.

The dirt quickly turned to mud. My friends screamed. The water wouldn't stop spraying. Tiny grass seeds swirled in small puddles.

"Follow me!" I started towards the sliding door to the family room, then thought of the new carpet. We had to go in through the garage.

"This way!" I changed direction and raced towards the side of the house, where Alex had been planting what I now knew where daffodil bulbs. My sneakers slid out from under me. I tumbled to the slimy ground and landed with a *splat*! Mud oozed through my short black skirt.

"Gross!" Fiona shrieked.

I scrambled up. No one else had fallen, but they were all soaked and dotted with dirt. Water sprayed everywhere.

"This way!" I cried again, running into the open garage and leading them away from the crazy sprinklers.

"I'm sopping wet!" Roseann cried. "What's happening?"

I had no idea.

But it was nothing good.

CHAPTER 13

Alex stood in the garage. His eyes grew huge at the sight of us. "Oh, wow. Are you okay? I'm so sorry. That was a huge mistake."

"You—you think?" I sputtered. My mud-caked skirt hardened to my thighs. Drops of dirty water ran down my arms and legs. "*Why* did you do that?"

"I'm sorry. All of you, I'm really sorry." Alex's face flamed. "I was getting Mom's chores done. I came out here." He pointed to a plastic box with a dial and a bunch of buttons hanging on the garage wall. "I've never worked the sprinkler system before. I was going to water the front yard while you guys were in the back."

"And you messed up," I guessed. Our shoes left a jumble of wet prints on the garage's concrete floor.

"You could say that." Alex shrugged sheepishly. "There were so many little buttons, so I figured it was easiest to hit the 'All System' switch. I'm guessing now that one means—"

"All the sprinklers!" I finished. "Every single one of them!"

"Stay there. I'll get towels!" Alex disappeared into the house.

"Look at us!" Miranda began to giggle.

"It's not funny," Roseann said. "I'm a mess! My shirt is a mess! And we have to wear them *tomorrow*!"

Everyone inspected the water and dirt on their silky shirts. Mine was the worst. Streaks of mud swirled across the silky red top I'd borrowed from Roseann.

"I'm sorry," I said. "I'll clean it. I promise."

"Lauren's going to be really upset," Roseann replied.

I didn't know what else to say. Once again, I'd messed up. I should have never been on the dirt. I prayed Mom's grass seeds hadn't completely floated away. I hoped mud came out of silk.

Why were things like this always happening to me? I looked at everyone's unhappy faces.

"Oooh!" I used the same spooky voice as I'd used on Shrimp's brother. "I am the mud monster. Watch me do the mud monster mash!" I whipped my wet hair around, sending droplets across the garage.

"Molly, stop!" Grace cried. "You're getting us even wetter."

"I can't stop," I moaned, walking stiffly like a mud monster. I'd hoped to make everyone laugh. No one did.

I stopped. "Just trying to find the funny side of it," I explained sheepishly.

"I know the sprinklers weren't your fault," Roseann said. "But it's not funny."

"I got the worst of it." I twirled. "I look like my bottom half was dipped in mud."

"Like a soft-serve cone," Miranda supplied. "Chocolate dipped."

"Exactly!" I cried. Miranda giggled with me. I wished Roseann could find it funny too.

Alex reappeared with towels. I offered to lend dry clothes, but no one was too bad off. *I* desperately needed a shower, though.

"We can practice more inside after I rinse," I offered.

"Oh, no!" Alex said. "No more practicing. I have to drive you to gymnastics."

"I'm going late today." I shot him my most meaningful look. With a little more time, I could smooth everything out.

Alex either didn't get my silent message or chose to ignore it. "I need to drop you off when it starts. Mom is going to be mega-upset about the yard when she gets home. I don't want to add something else."

"That's your problem. You ran the sprinklers. You ate the cupcakes," I reminded him.

"You allowed all your friends to dance on the grass seed," he countered.

I did. We were in this together.

"I just texted my mom," Grace said. "She's coming soon."

"Me too," Fiona added.

"We can figure out different tops to wear tomorrow if these don't wash out," Roseann offered. "The dance was done anyhow. I think we're good to go."

I turned on the TV in the family room. Everyone laid towels on the rug and sprawled out while I took the world's fastest shower and pulled on my red leotard.

I hurried down the stairs. Chrissy Bleeker stood in the hall, talking to Alex.

"Hey, Molly." Chrissy grinned like we were old friends. She wore a neon-yellow hoodie, her field hockey skirt, and sneakers. "Roseann texted that you had a washout. I came to get her."

"Crazy, right?" I grinned back. "You should've seen my legs."

"Always lots of excitement with you," she remarked.

"You don't know the half of it." Alex said. He stood awkwardly.

"Hey, how's Myrtle?" I asked.

"Excellent. You should visit her again," Chrissy offered. "With . . . what was the name? Captain Hook?"

"I'm thinking Captain Hook and Myrtle are better off having a long-distance relationship. He'll just watch Myrtle from afar."

"Who's Myrtle?" Alex asked.

"Chrissy's best friend," I replied.

"Really? I'd like to meet her," Alex said, overly enthusiastic.

"You may not like her. She's a little stiff. She can be a real stick-in-the-mud." I chuckled. So did Chrissy.

"What?" Alex said, looking between me and Chrissy.

I left her to explain as I stepped into the family room. All the girls had their backs to me, talking and watching the TV. I paused in the doorway and listened to the natural way they finished one another's sentences. Anna had come up with a new top option. Roseann thought we should bow, one by one, at the end. Miranda wanted to review the dance steps, and Roseann used her fingers on the floor to show her where to go.

I didn't speak or let them know I was there. Even

though this was my house and these were my friends, I felt oddly as if I were intruding.

I'm not really *part of the group,* I realized. Not yet. Unlike with Eden, Roseann didn't miss me when I left the room. Would that time ever come?

Suddenly I was tired of working so hard at the Roseann Project.

"Alex," I said, returning to the hall. "Time to go."

"We should really wait for everyone to get picked up." Alex spoke to me but gazed at Chrissy.

"You said I can't be late." More than anything, I wanted to escape to my room and crawl under my comforter. Since that wasn't going to happen with everyone sprawled in my family room, I'd go to the gym. Anywhere but here.

Alex continued to give Chrissy a goofy grin.

"I could wait here with the girls until their rides come, while you run Molly to the gym," Chrissy offered.

"Really? But will you stay until I get back?" he asked. "Stay here, I mean."

I rolled my eyes. Now I could see what was happening. Alex was so crushing on Roseann's sister!

"Definitely," she agreed. She wandered into the family room and sat on the sofa with her long legs tucked behind her.

"Let's go!" Alex grabbed his keys off the front hall bench and nearly sprinted for the car.

I glanced back. No one had come looking for me. I wished Eden was here to tell me how to make things right with Roseann. Grabbing my gym bag, I followed Alex out the door without saying good-bye.

"You made a mistake," I insisted after the warm-up and stretching. "I'm not supposed to be in this group." I waved my arms towards the girls in red leotards around me, most of who were in elementary school.

"It's not a mistake," Nastia said, her arms crossed. "This is where you belong."

"No, it's not," I protested. Nastia had bumped me down another group. A lump rose in my throat as I tried to figure it out.

"We need to strengthen your fundamentals. No more sloppy! Sharpen your focus. Tighten your body. Commit to practice *every* day. Until that happens, this level is best." Nastia's tone was clipped, and she turned away from me. "Over to the beam, all of you."

As I followed, I gazed longingly at Sofia and her group lining up to vault. Sofia shot me a look of pity. Since she'd met me, I'd been pulled down two levels. If

I continued at this pace, I'd be doing somersaults with the toddlers by next week!

"Handstands," Nastia called. "First on small beam. If I like your position, you move to the big beam."

We lined up in front of several low beams only an inch off the mats. Nastia clapped loudly. Together we placed our hands on the beam and kicked up into split handstands.

"Weight on fingertips, not palms!" Nastia called, walking among us. "Straight body! Slowly move your legs together."

Upside down, I concentrated on not arching my back and on squaring my hips. With her hand, Nastia tried to push each of us over. To each girl who wobbled or fell, she barked, "Tighter!"

Nastia made us lunge up to a handstand on the small beam many times before graduating us to the big beam.

"Focus!" she called again and again.

The cheerleaders' chants floated over the wall. Music stopped and started for the girls practicing floor routines. Their feet thumped as they stuck the landings of their tumbling passes. I couldn't block out the noise. I couldn't focus on tightening and straightening my body. I wanted to twist and flip. I wanted to move to the music, the way I had for years at Daria's gym. My feet flopped down, and I jumped off the beam.

"I have to go to the bathroom," I told Nastia. She scowled before letting me go.

Once again, I sat alone on the bench in the empty locker room. I fixed my ponytail, digging out the bits of dirt I'd failed to wash out. I'd need another shower later. I hoped Mom would agree to blow my hair straight for the talent show tomorrow.

Everything would be okay with Roseann, I decided as I replayed the afternoon in my head. She hadn't been mad at me. In fact, she'd been quite nice about the mud on the shirt and getting all wet. I was the one who overreacted. Just because she didn't know I was standing silently behind her was no reason to run off.

I'd text her when I got home and say sorry. I could fix this.

I stood to go back to the gym, but my feet took me towards the cheerleading door. A strong urge made me want to peek again. Slowly I slipped inside and squatted by the same pile of mats I'd hidden behind before. The tall cheer coach was out on the floor, too busy spotting stunts to notice me. I watched the cheerleaders and grinned when I recognized Shrimp. She had an enormous purple-sequined bow in her high ponytail.

"Let me see full extensions, group by group," the coach

called. She moved to Shrimp's group. "Ready, okay!"

Shrimp stepped her feet into the cupped hands of two girls facing each other. Another girl stood behind and supported the wrists of the two girls. The girl in the back counted out the beats, as the girls raised Shrimp halfway, and then all the way, into the air. Shrimp stood tall, extending her arms in a wide V. She smiled widely too, her braces glinting against the bright lights.

She looked amazing, towering high above the squad. She completely trusted the girls who held her. They kept their eyes glued on Shrimp, watching out for her. Then I noticed the slight tremble in the arms of one of the girls on the bottom. The coach noticed it too.

"Ready, okay, and . . . down!" she called.

The girls on the bottom popped Shrimp into the air. She flew, folding gracefully into a pike position, and landed safely into the cradle of the girls' arms. "Whoo-hoo!" the four cheered together, pumping their fists and jumping.

"What's shakin', bacon?" Shrimp nudged the girl whose arms had trembled.

"My arms!" The girl began to laugh at herself, and the others joined in. Even the coach laughed.

"Okay, we're going up again," the coach said. "Shannon, put those arms into lockdown mode this time."

As I watched Shrimp sail into the sky supported by Shannon and the other girls, I realized that gymnastics was no longer fun. It never had been at Andre's gym. And I certainly wasn't going to the Olympics or even training for it, no matter how hard I worked. I had to find the courage to tell Mom that Top Flight wasn't the place for me. Simple as that. I couldn't keep hiding and pretending.

The girls cradled Shrimp on the release. As the coach moved to the next group, she glanced over her shoulder and noticed me. She winked. Embarrassed, I scurried back into the locker room and then into the gym.

My eyes roamed the huge room and all the red leotards. My new group was no longer by the beam. Where was I supposed to be? Along the far wall, a neon-yellow hoodie stood out in the sea of red. I blinked, then looked again.

Was that Chrissy Bleeker?

My brother, Alex, stood next to her. What were they doing *here*? Why were they *together*?

My brain whirled as my gaze landed on a girl standing next to Chrissy. I caught my breath. Roseann!

Roseann was here!

CHAPTER 14

She'd come all the way down to apologize, I realized. How awesome was that?

My heart soared. She'd showed up without Grace, Miranda, and the others. Just the two of us. Together. True friends. I couldn't help but smile.

I stepped forwards, then paused. She held something. What was it? I squinted.

The pink notebook lay open in her hands. And she was writing furiously in it.

What was she writing? I wondered. More background information?

What I saw next caused my smile to fade and my lungs to tighten. Andre walked towards them. In less than a minute, he'd be standing in front of Roseann and her reporter's notebook. And then she'd ask him questions about me. About—

I couldn't let that happen. I had to tell her that it had

all been a misunderstanding. I had to tell her *now*.

I sprinted straight across the gym and over the floor-routine mats. "Watch out!" I called, inches away from colliding with Sofia as she landed her tumbling pass.

"Molly!" she screamed, startled. Her legs wobbled.

"Sorry." I couldn't stop. I had to get to Roseann.

Panting, I dodged between Andre and Roseann. "Hi, Andre. This is my brother and my friend."

"Everything is okay?" he asked.

"Hi, are you—?" Roseann began.

"Totally fine," I assured Andre, cutting her off. "I'll be back out there in a sec."

"Quickly," he reminded me before heading towards the vault to watch Kelsey warm up front handspring–front twists.

"What are you doing here?" I asked Alex.

"Roseann wanted to see where you did gymnastics, so I took her and Chrissy on a field trip."

"A field trip? Here?"

"Hi, Molly!" Roseann greeted me brightly. "I was looking for you out there. I wanted to see you do something, so I could describe it in the article."

"Molly is really good," Alex bragged to Chrissy. "She does all these crazy flips."

I rolled my eyes. He was only praising me to get her attention.

"Alex, don't you have a library or someplace to go to?" I asked pointedly.

"Nope. I'm good to hang out." He acted as if he were always this mellow, which he so wasn't. "Hey, when you finish, I could drive you and Roseann for ice cream."

I stared at him. Crushing on Chrissy had turned him into alien brother. Ice cream? Really? This was the first time since he had gotten his driver's license that he'd offered to take me for ice cream.

"That's great," Chrissy answered for me.

"So, Molly, can I talk to your coach?" Roseann asked. "That was him before? The blond guy?"

"Now's not a good time." I flexed my toes as if about to spring into a tuck. "There's something you don't have right . . . something I need to tell you. . . ."

"If I can't talk to him, can I see your Olympic routine?" She swiveled about, searching the gym. "Who else here is going to the Olympics with you? What about that girl Kelsey?"

"Seriously? Seriously?" Sofia repeated. I hadn't heard her come up behind me. Her voice sounded incredulous.

"Hey, Sofia," I said softly. "I'm sorry about before."

“You think that Molly is going to the Olympics?” Sofia asked Roseann.

“Well, yeah. She said that—”

“She told you that? She told you that she is as good as Kelsey?” Sofia’s voice grew louder with each question. “Molly told you that she is working on a routine for the upcoming *Olympics*?”

I didn’t have to turn to know that all activity in the gym had stopped. Every gymnast halted her extensions and body tightening to listen.

All their eyes bored into my back. My face turned redder than my leotard.

I glanced over my shoulder. A few cheerleaders peeked through the locker-room door. Was that Shrimp’s giant purple bow? The tall cheer coach appeared, waving them inside. I whirled back around, embarrassed.

“Molly?” Roseann asked. Confusion clouded her face.

“I’m not going to this Olympics,” I admitted.

“*This* Olympics? Don’t think I’m being mean, Molly, but you’re dreaming,” Sofia said.

“I didn’t mean this one. That came out wrong. Roseann, I’m not going to the Olympics. Ever,” I said quietly.

“What are you talking about?” Roseann demanded.

"It was a misunderstanding." I wished so many people weren't listening.

"But you told me you were going to be a world champion."

"No, I didn't. You said that," I protested.

"Even if that's true, you didn't correct me," Roseann countered. "Ever!"

"I tried to. Kind of. It's just that . . . I thought we'd laugh about it later. A joke, you know?" I said feebly.

"A joke? I don't get your humor, Molly. You think everything's funny. Do you think it would've been funny if I'd handed in this article?" Roseann cried. "Newspapers are supposed to report the truth!"

"I wasn't going to let you do that," I admitted. "I swear I was going to stop you today."

"Today? Why not last week, before I begged Mrs. Murphy to let me write about you? Or this week, when you knew I was working so hard on the article?"

Tears stung my eyes. How could I explain to Roseann how much I'd wanted to be her friend? How I'd picked her out on that very first day? How I'd been so afraid I'd mess up everything by telling her?

"I'm so sorry," I said. "Maybe we could just switch the article a bit. I'll talk to Mrs. Murphy. I'll tell her it was my fault."

"Forget it, Molly." Roseann turned to Chrissy. "I want to go home."

"Sorry. I think we should leave," Chrissy said to Alex. He'd been staring at me this whole time, his expression changing from amusement to sympathy. Roseann headed towards the door.

"Sure, no problem." Alex jumped to attention when Chrissy followed Roseann. "Molly, you coming?"

I glanced behind me again. At some point, Sofia had left my side and returned to the floor. Now she ran through her front handspring–front tuck. All the other gymnasts were back to the bars or vault or whatever they'd been doing before. No cheerleaders remained. Even though no one was watching me, I concentrated hard to keep back my tears.

"Molly?" Alex called.

Andre appeared by my side. "Practice is not over yet," he said to Alex. "You come back in thirty minutes, yes? Moll-le, you go to beam."

I didn't move. I stared into Andre's ice-blue eyes, willing him to see that I needed a hug and not a front walkover. He didn't get it. Not the way Daria would have. Not the way Eden would have.

I watched Sofia split-leap across the mats, so into her own routine. Then I gazed at Roseann, tapping her foot by the door where she and Chrissy waited. Which would be worse—staying at the gym or sitting next to Roseann in the back seat?

I groaned. How did I create such a colossal mess?

I followed Alex to the car, leaving Andre and the gym behind. I didn't belong in this gym. I had known that days ago. Maybe my friendship with Roseann could still be fixed.

Roseann spent the car ride home staring out the window. She wouldn't look at me or talk to me. The only time she spoke was when Chrissy asked, "Should we stop for ice cream?"

"Definitely not," Roseann said.

"I'm sorry," I said again, quietly, so only she could hear.

Roseann didn't answer.

The airline ticket rested on top of my large canvas duffel bag the next morning. Inside I'd packed two pairs of pajamas and many different changes of clothes. Almost half of my closet. I was all ready to go. Picking up my phone, I reread the texts Eden and I had sent late last night.

guess what????

what???

Im comin 2morrow

here????

yes!!!! Flyin in 4 wkend

OMG!!!!! happy dance!!!!! & guess what?
we have 1/2 day skool!

can I sleep over?

yes!! y r u comin???

dad wants me 2 visit

XCELLENT! Darias w_me on Sat??

def!

cant w8 to C U!!!!

me 2!!

Last night, I'd tossed and turned and twisted up my blankets, trying to fall asleep. Finally, at midnight, I'd crawled out of bed to sit at my desk. In the dark, I stared at the ticket on my bulletin board. The answer to my problem was right in front of me. I'd go to Arizona for the weekend!

I had the ticket. Plus Dad had said I could come anytime. Eden was still awake, and we texted. I packed my cutest outfits. I was totally pumped. Now that I had started thinking about going, I couldn't stop.

All I had to do was call Dad.

And tell Mom. But she was fast asleep.

I dialed Dad's number on my cell, but I didn't press Send.

I wasn't sure what exactly to say to him. I wanted to ask him if I could stay. Not just for the weekend. Stay forever. I'd slip right back into school, Daria's gym, and my group of friends, as if I'd only been on vacation. I'd ask Carmen to bring me to the barn to meet Buddy. Maybe I'd finally ride a horse. It was the perfect plan.

I crept back into bed without calling. Should I ask him now or after the plane had landed? I fell asleep before I could decide.

* * *

Now I sat cross-legged on my bedroom floor and dialed Dad.

"Hello?" His voice sounded heavy with sleep.

I groaned. I'd forgotten it was four o'clock in the morning there. "Hi, Dad, it's me."

"Molly? What's wrong?" he cried, startled and confused. "Who's hurt?"

"No one's hurt. I'm sorry it's so early. I wanted to talk to you." I tried to be extrapeppy to make up for the early hour. "I'm going to use that plane ticket you gave me to visit you!"

"Hmmm, that's great." He yawned. I heard him fumble around on his nightstand for his glasses. "Why don't we talk about that idea later today?"

"That's just it. I'm coming *today*. I went online and checked the airline. A flight leaves this morning and lands early afternoon. You can pick me up at the airport, right?"

"What?" Now he sounded fully awake. "Today? What's going on there? Are you okay?"

"I'm fine. I really miss you and Arizona. I want to see you," I said. "Please?" I wasn't lying. I did miss him.

"Well . . . sure. Okay. A visit is good." He paused. "Your mom is on board with this sudden plan?"

"Totally." That was a lie. I hadn't told Mom . . . yet.

I'd been working up the nerve—and giving her time for her morning coffee. I needed a ride to the airport and for her to say yes, and there was no chance of either happening precoffee. Plus, if Dad said yes first, maybe that would help convince her.

"Okay, then, a weekend visit. What time do you and Alex arrive?" he asked.

"Not Alex. Just me." My voice quavered as I pushed on. "And Dad? I was thinking I'd stay longer than a weekend. Wouldn't it be great if I lived with you? I could ride horses with Carmen, and I'd be a real help around the house."

Dad said nothing for the longest time, and for a moment, I feared he'd fallen back to sleep.

"Molly, honey, what's going on there?" he asked finally. "You know the arrangement your mom and I have. You and Alex live with her. It's not that I don't want you and love you, but I travel all the time for my business, and Carmen is a flight attendant. We're just not home enough."

"Yeah, but, maybe there's a way—" I tried.

"Whoa, Molly. I'm not awake enough for this conversation. I don't know why you want to leave your mom—"

"I don't want to leave her," I interrupted him.

"Molly, I promise I will help you solve whatever problem you are having, but jumping on a plane may not be the answer," he cautioned.

"You don't know that," I said.

He sighed. "I don't. Let me think on it and talk to your mom. Hang tight for bit, honey. I love you."

We said good-bye. A minute later, the house phone rang. I knew Dad was calling Mom. Now I wished I'd talked with her first.

I inspected the ticket. I couldn't imagine abandoning Mom. She cut my fruit the way I liked it. We snuggled on the sofa together at night with cookie-dough ice cream and watched food reality shows. She could tell when I needed a hug and when I needed to be left alone. Dad was often more fun than Mom, but he didn't know any of that.

I didn't really want to live with Dad and Carmen.

I just didn't want to go to Hillsbury Middle School today.

Or ever.

What I wanted was to live with Mom and Alex, but not here.

My phone buzzed. A group message sent by Anna.

Remember—black skirt, black tank,

black flats, blow-out hair, and dark red lipstick!!!

Had Roseann not told Anna what had happened? Was I still part of the group? I watched as Grace, Fiona, Miranda, and Roseann texted that they agreed.

Molly? Do u have all? Anna texted the group when I didn't respond.

I'd assumed Roseann had kicked me out by now. I twisted my silver ring nervously. Should I tell them I wasn't showing up for the talent show? That I was flying to Arizona?

I have an xtra black tank if u need, Roseann texted the group.

Don't need, I texted back.

Tonight I'd see Eden. Lying in her trundle bed with her old smiley-face comforter wrapped around me in the dark, I'd tell her what had happened with Roseann. All of it. Eden would know what to do. Maybe her mom had written a blog about it.

"Running out on me?" Mom poked her head in my doorway. Her cheeriness sounded forced. "Flying off?"

"No. I just thought I'd visit Dad."

Looking suspiciously at my packed bag, she kicked off her heels, then sat next to me on my rug. "What's wrong?"

"Nothing." I made my voice sound casual. "Dad gave me the ticket. He said I could use it whenever I wanted. I want to go now. Dad said it was okay."

"He said you wanted to stay longer. A lot longer."

I heard the hurt in her voice and felt horrible. "It was just a silly thought. I don't want to leave you. It has nothing to do with you. Really." I gulped. "Can I go for the weekend?"

"Molly, I think it's great that you want to see your dad." She spoke softly. "I would never stop you. I just wish you'd spoken to me first before rushing ahead."

I grimaced. "I do that a lot. Rush ahead."

"You do," Mom agreed.

"Can I go? The plane leaves soon. I'm all packed."

Mom pressed her fingertips together. "You can't miss school."

"But . . ." I thought about telling her some other story to convince her. Then, without warning, the whole horrible Roseann Project–Olympics story tumbled out.

Mom gathered me in her arms, and I pressed my face against her soft sweater. "Making friends is hard, Molly. I know. Do you realize I haven't met anyone outside my office yet?"

"We should hang out together," I joked halfheartedly.

"I'd like that." She gave me a reassuring squeeze.

I hadn't realized that Mom was having a hard time too. Now that I thought about it, I wasn't the only one who had left folks behind in Arizona. My mom had given up my aunt Kelly and her friend Lora in the move.

"Why'd you move us if we had to leave the people we liked?" I asked. "I mean, I know you got the good job and all, but . . ."

"The job is a big thing, Molly. Big financially and big for me." She twirled a strand of her hair, silent for a moment. "I needed a fresh start. Since your dad left, I'd been stuck. He moved forwards. He found Carmen. I needed to jump-start my life, and I had to make a big change to do that."

"You didn't even ask me," I said quietly.

"I know. I made a selfish choice, but I really think it will be good for our family. Alex seems to really like it here. I hope, in time, you will too." She scratched my back exactly where it feels best. "We both have to give it some time."

"I can't face Roseann today," I confessed.

"Running away from your problems isn't the answer. Roseann sounds like a nice girl. I'm sure she'll get over this."

"That's why I should wait until Monday," I insisted.

"It'll be better then."

"You're tougher than you think, Molly," she promised me.

"Everything is harder here."

"You're growing up. Everything is harder no matter where you live," Mom said.

"So can I miss school today?" I asked again.

"You agreed to be part of their dance group. Isn't the dance now choreographed for six people?" she pointed out.

"Yeah, but they can change it back. They don't need me." I played with the zipper of my duffel. "She might never want to be my friend again, you know."

Mom nodded. "That's a possibility. You won't know if you hide from her. A friendship is built on trust. You need to give her a reason to trust you."

I groaned and continued to pull the zipper open and closed.

"Today's talent show isn't only about Roseann," she reminded me. "All those other girls are waiting on you too."

I thought of Miranda. She needed me alongside her to keep up. Plus, she smiled at my jokes. Sometimes.

"How's this? You go be fabulous in that talent show. I'll have Alex pick you up after school and drive you to the airport for a quick trip to see your dad. And Eden," she said knowingly.

"I can go back home?"

"This is home, Molly. Here. With me. But, yes, you can go to Arizona for the weekend. *After* school."

Mom's mind had been made up. I could live with that.

"That's great!" I wrapped her in a hug. "What about Andre?" I'd told her how Andre's gym made me feel so alone and bad at gymnastics.

"Let me call him this afternoon. I'll sort out the money part somehow."

"I'm sorry."

"Mistakes happen." She kissed my forehead. "I'll also drop the red silk shirt at the dry cleaners. But when you get back, you and Alex are replanting the grass seed—and doing a whole lot more yard work."

"I kind of figured that." I grimaced. "Hey, how about I plant it now instead of going to school?"

"Good try, but no."

"I figured that too."

"Listen, sweetie, if things don't work with Roseann, there are other girls in your school, you know," Mom said.

"I know, but I'm going to handle this." I stood.

"I'm proud of you." She stood too. "Be ready in ten minutes?"

"Do you have dark red lipstick I can borrow?" I asked, rummaging in my drawer for a black tank.

"Dark red? Wow!" She seemed surprised. "Isn't that a bit much?"

"You said I should—"

"No, dark red is fine." She stepped into the hall, then turned. "I have this strong feeling that everything is going to turn around, and you'll have so much fun today."

"I hope so." I thought about the apologies I needed to make—to Kate, to Mrs. Murphy, and to Roseann again. Not my definition of fun.

"Bring your bag. I'll call your dad and talk with Alex. Meet you downstairs." She headed off.

"Hey, Mom! I might need more than ten minutes." I shook out my long curls. "I have to blow my mane straight."

"Now?" she cried. "Why?"

"There's a photo," I explained. "If I'm going, Roseann says I've got to look good!"

CHAPTER 15

"Is my lipstick crooked?" Miranda gave me a lopsided grin.

"Not at all." I glanced around backstage. All the kids in the talent show had gathered to get ready. A girl tuned her cello. A girl in a tutu laced her pointe shoes. A boy juggled fruit. The green apple kept falling and rolling. Our group, in all black with the pop of bright color on our lips, looked the most grown-up and sleek.

First period had been cancelled. Through the thick velvet curtains I heard muffled voices, as the rest of the sixth graders filed into the auditorium. Backstage buzzed with nerves and excitement.

"Onyx? Is that your name?" Ms. Fairley adjusted her glasses and checked her clipboard.

"Yep, that's us," Grace said proudly. "Do you get it? Onyx is a gemstone that's black."

"And you're wearing all black," Ms. Fairley said. "I

got it. All group members here?"

"All here," Grace agreed.

I glanced at Roseann. She didn't look away, but she didn't smile either. She'd been nice enough since I'd arrived, just not overly so. She obviously hadn't told the others what had happened. If she had, I was sure Grace would've said something.

I couldn't figure out why she kept it a secret. I'd assumed she'd texted them as soon as Alex had dropped her and Chrissy home.

"Your group is up next for your photo." Ms. Fairley pointed to a bearded man with a camera and tall lights in a far corner. "After the photo, it's your turn to perform. We need to stay on schedule."

We nodded, and Ms. Fairley left to check in with the other talent show performers.

"I think we all look great." Roseann straightened her black headband and smoothed her hair. "Don't you?"

"Totally," Anna agreed. "Hands in?"

We reached our hands into the circle, the same way we'd done at field hockey.

"Wait a sec." I cleared my throat and forced my voice to sound normal. "There's something I need to tell all of you."

I explained that I wasn't going to the Olympics. I

told them that I'd been flattered they thought I was that good, but I wasn't, even though I desperately wished I was. I said I'd been terribly wrong not to correct them.

"I don't get it," Miranda said. "Why would you say that in the first place?"

Like her, they were all more confused than angry. Roseann watched me. Her face didn't reveal her feelings.

"It's hard to explain," I said. I thought about telling them that, technically, I hadn't been the one to say that I was going to the Olympics, but that hadn't gone over well with Roseann last night.

"Is any of it true?" Grace asked.

"Any what?"

"Anything about you," she said skeptically.

"Everything else is. Totally! I promise."

"Onyx!" Ms. Fairley called, saving me. "Photo time."

As we popped our hands up together, I felt them all glance sideways at me. Probably wondering if I was really from Arizona or if I really was a gymnast.

Bob, the photographer, lined us up. Grace, Fiona, Anna, and Roseann kneeling in front. Miranda and me standing behind them. We waited silently for our picture to be taken. I stared at the back of Roseann's head. Would she let this pass? Would she ever laugh about it?

Her head didn't give me any answers. My stomach tightened with dread. *If only I could press a reset button and start again,* I thought.

"Girls, everyone's looking a bit stiff. Show me more natural smiles. How about on three we all say 'cheese'?" Bob asked with an exaggerated grin.

"How about 'meow'?" I joked back, needing to break the tension. "We look more like black cats than mice."

"We're not saying that," Grace whispered up at me.

"Just trying to get everyone to smile," I said.

"Meow?" Bob offered.

No one but me meowed back.

"Okay, no takers for 'meow.' How about 'Onyx' on three?" Bob didn't wait for an answer this time. "One . . . two . . . three."

"Onyx!" we all cried. I extended the *X* sound for a long time, giving my biggest smile. "We sound like snakes," I quipped, suddenly nervous around these girls.

"Be serious," Grace said to me. "Can we take another?" she asked Bob.

"Let's try that again." Bob raised his camera. "Give me a happy thought."

Roseann whirled around. "Don't be silly, Molly."

"One . . . two . . ." Bob began the count.

"What's wrong with being silly?" I asked.

"Let's just take the photo," Fiona said.

Several kids grouped behind Bob, watching us. Impulsively, I put two fingers up on both my hands and gave Anna and Grace bunny ears.

"Darling!" Bob called. "I see that. Hands down."

"Seriously, Molly," Grace muttered as the kids behind Bob giggled. "This photo is going on the wall."

"Ready?" Bob said.

The girls all posed with one hand on their hips. I puffed out my cheeks and crossed my eyes. The kids facing us laughed loudly this time. I didn't care that they were laughing at me. Laughter was better than the serious silence of the photo.

"Molly, stop it," Roseann said tightly.

"Okay, okay," I agreed. Suddenly I felt bad. I'd gotten carried away again. This wasn't the way to win Roseann back. I vowed to smile sweetly from now on and do nothing else. "I'm done. Let's do this."

"One . . . two . . ." Bob started the count again. We all smiled and posed.

On three, a tiny girl in a dark green glittery leotard sailed into the picture.

"Photo bomb!" Shrimp cried, popping her smiling

face in between me and Miranda.

I cracked up.

I laughed so hard that I started my weird hiccup thing. Shrimp grabbed my hands, and we tumbled to the floor. Then she started to hiccup too!

"Hysterical!" I choked out, still hiccupping. "I love photo bombs."

"Onyx, they're calling you onto the stage." Ms. Fairley hurried over to us. "Now!"

I hiccupped loudly. Shrimp echoed me.

"You have to stop that," Grace said.

I stood and hiccupped some more. "I can't. No one will notice."

"Yes, they will," Roseann insisted. She and Grace shared a nervous glance.

"Okay." I hiccupped again. "So they will. Who cares? We're dancing and not singing, right?"

"Singing would be funny." Shrimp hiccupped twice as loudly as I did, as she tried to sing "Happy Birthday."

"I care," Roseann said as the announcer called Onyx's name again. The audience had quieted, waiting for us to appear. Roseann's eyes darted nervously towards the stage. Then her gaze settled on me.

I took a deep breath and held it, willing away the hiccups. Once again, my silliness had upset Roseann.

I didn't want to keep upsetting her. I wished I could figure out the secret to making us click. Why was it so hard?

As another hiccup escaped, I clapped my hand over my mouth. "I can't stop."

"I don't think you can go on with us," Grace said.

I looked to Fiona. She nodded. Miranda and Anna examined the floor, not saying anything.

I should've found a way to get on that plane this morning, I thought. I hadn't fixed anything with Roseann.

"That's fine," Shrimp said suddenly. "Molly changed groups."

"I did?" I turned to her.

"Yes," Shrimp announced, not bothering to hide her hiccups. "You're with me."

"Onyx!" Ms. Fairley said sternly. "Now or never?"

"Molly?" Roseann asked uncomfortably.

"Can you do the dance okay without me?" I hiccupped again.

"Yes," Roseann said. "We can. But I don't want you to be upset—"

"Then I'm with Shrimp." I wrapped my arm around her tiny shoulder.

Roseann nodded.

"So you two are together?" Ms. Fairley asked, after Onyx ran onstage and the familiar beat of their music started up.

"We are." Shrimp slung her arm over my shoulder.

"Bob, I need you to snap a photo of these two," Ms. Fairley called.

Bob jumped in front of us, camera ready. "One . . . two . . ."

On three, I gave Shrimp bunny ears, and she gave them to me. We both puffed out our cheeks and crossed our eyes.

"How about a more serious one, girls?" Bob asked.

"Nah," Shrimp said. "Unless you want?"

"Never," I said. "Hey, our hiccups went away."

Together, from the wings, we watched Onyx dance. I nodded along, silently cheering as Miranda remembered all the moves and didn't knock into Grace. Roseann looked prettier than ever. Miranda had moved up, so they were all in one line. No one in the audience realized I was missing.

Or that I'd ever been part of their group at all.

"Thanks," I said to Shrimp.

"For what?"

"For jumping in when I needed you."

"Happy to help, sea kelp."

Ms. Fairley tapped our shoulders. "Two acts, then you're on, girls."

"What are we doing out there?" I asked Shrimp. Suddenly the stage looked large and the audience even larger.

"Tumbling. Don't worry, we'll figure it out." She gazed at my black skirt, lipstick, and straight hair. "You're going to have to change, if we're going to flip."

Shrimp's sparkly green leotard gave me an idea. "I have just the thing. Wait here!"

Racing to the far corner of backstage, I found my duffel bag tucked behind a trunk overflowing with sombreros, cowboy hats, jester caps, and other hats used for school shows. My weekend bag had been way too large to squeeze into my locker. I was already late when Mom dropped me off. Mrs. Murphy saw me struggling and told me to bring it to the talent show. Now I dug around inside.

Hiding behind a scuffed armoire and a screen with the silhouette of a city skyline painted on it, I pushed off my shoes and changed outfits. Then I pulled my hair into a ponytail. I ran back to Shrimp.

"That's the way, blue jay!" she called when she saw my lavender leotard with the rhinestone sunburst design. I'd packed it to wear with Eden to Daria's gym.

"Do you ever run out of those sayings?" I asked.

Shrimp shrugged. "I guess you'll have to hang out with me to find out."

"They're setting up for you two now," Ms. Fairley said as the curtain closed on Lyla playing a guitar and singing. Roseann and crew had left the stage earlier, to tons of applause. They stood together in the wings, watching Lyla. I caught Roseann's eye and gave her a smile. I wanted her to know that I wasn't upset.

Ms. Fairley placed her hand on my shoulder as four boys pulled mats onto the stage. She looked from Roseann to Shrimp to me. "Molly, is everything fine?"

I could see how she'd be confused.

"All good," I said, "except I don't know what I'm supposed to do out there. Shrimp, I don't know the routine. I don't know the steps."

"There are no steps. Follow the music." Shrimp grabbed my hand and squeezed it. "We'll make it up together."

"Girls, they're about to announce you." Ms. Fairley's cell phone buzzed. She was using it to text with the guy doing the lighting and the announcing. "Wait! What's your group name?"

"We're the Olympic Tumblers," Shrimp declared.

"What?" I cried.

"You wanted to be part of the Olympics, didn't you?" Shrimp shot me a mischievous grin. "That's how I heard it that day at the gym."

"You heard?" I cringed. I thought I'd spied Shrimp's purple bow.

"If Coach hadn't dragged me away, I would've stood up for you. Sofia should chill out. I mean, obviously, it was a joke."

"Well, it's not exactly how it started. The truth is—"

"You can tell me later, if you want." Shrimp nodded to the rising curtain. "Are you ready?"

"So the Olympic Tumblers? That's who you are?" Ms. Fairley asked impatiently.

"That's who *we* are," I agreed.

The opening notes of the Two Hearts song blared out as the announcer called, "Give it up for the Olympic Tumblers!"

Shrimp looked at me. "Ready?"

"Ready, Freddy!" I cried.

"Good one." Shrimp nodded, and together we ran out. We turned a roundoff and launched into two back handsprings, side by side. I don't know how we both knew to do them, but we did.

We continued to tumble. Sometimes we did the same stunts at the same time. Sometimes she flipped and I danced, and then I flipped and she danced. The beat of the music guided my body. Shrimp seemed to hear the music the same way I did. We moved together. We used moves we'd made up on her trampoline. High-flying split jumps. Full-body shimmies. Even that cool dance move she'd showed me through the fence.

A bunch of times, one of us would do a crazy shake or a ridiculous twist that would crack the other up. From different sides of the stage, we handspringed towards the middle. When our feet touched, we pretended to bump. We tumbled to the ground, clownlike. The audience laughed with us.

What an amazing sound!

Soon I forgot the entire sixth grade was watching. With the bright lights and the thumping music, I was mostly aware of Shrimp by my side. That wonderful sensation of flying through the air was back. I hadn't felt this free and easy since moving here. The minutes zoomed by, and when the song ended, I slid into a split and raised my arms. Shrimp did the same.

I want to do this again! I thought. Could we convince Ms. Fairley to have them replay our music? We'd make up a completely different, but equally fabulous, routine.

I was so into my own happy thoughts that I didn't register the noise at first. Slowly, though, the audience's clapping and cheering soaked in. The noise grew deafening.

I squinted into the lights, unsure I was seeing right. I turned to Shrimp.

"Standing O!" she mouthed to me, raising her arms into a circle above her head.

I gasped. They were giving us a standing ovation. Shrimp and I were a hit!

CHAPTER 16

I leaned against the planter outside the front doors to the school. All the buses had left, the walkers had scattered, and the car line had dwindled to one or two late parents. Alex still wasn't here. He'd texted that he had to talk to someone at his school, so I'd have to wait. *Must be a teacher thing,* I figured.

Now I was the last kid at school on a Friday afternoon.

I bent down, unzipped my bulging duffel bag, and pulled out a sweatshirt with a cool camouflage print. The sky was heavy with gray clouds, and a chill weighed down the late September sky. I shivered in my black tank. I'd had no choice but to put the Onyx outfit back on after the talent show. I couldn't walk around school in a leotard.

Everything had changed after Shrimp and I exited the stage. All day, kids came up and congratulated me.

The weird thing was that Shrimp and I hadn't even won. A girl who played the piano and sang a song from *Wicked* won. But Shrimp and I were clearly the audience favorite.

"You looked like you were having so much fun up there," Morgan, my partner in my math class, said wistfully.

"I was," I confided. "Lots of fun."

"We should hang out sometime after school," she suggested. "If that's okay."

"That's great!" I told her. I liked Morgan. She always had the coolest designs on her nails. She drew the flowers and snowflakes herself with special polish. She promised to do them on mine.

Morgan wasn't the only one who'd noticed me. I had met more kids today than in the past couple weeks. I felt, in a strange way, as if today was my first day.

I didn't see Roseann or Shrimp for the rest of the day. During lunch, I didn't go to the cafeteria, and I realized I was missing out on Sweets Friday. I'd forgotten to bring a treat anyway.

Instead, I found Mrs. Murphy eating a tuna sandwich in her classroom. I sat across from her and told her that I wasn't going to the Olympics. I apologized and tried to explain the best I could. She was really understanding.

She encouraged me to stay on the newspaper staff and even shared her potato chips. I showed her how to crumble them and put them inside her tuna sandwich. The crunchiness balanced the mushiness of the tuna. She agreed. She was going to see if her little son liked it when she got home.

I heard footsteps on the walkway behind me.

"Have a good weekend, Molly," Ms. Fairley said as she left the school with Miss Plaza, my science teacher. They both waved.

"Thanks! You too!" I called. The teachers now knew me here.

I pulled on my sweatshirt and zipped my duffel. Packing seemed like a lifetime ago. I watched as a girl about my age climbed out of the backseat of a blue car that had pulled into the parking lot a few minutes earlier. A man and a woman exited the front seat. I guessed they were her parents. She gazed around with a bewildered look.

Instantly, I recognized the look. I'd had that look too. She was new.

The front door pushed open behind me, and Mr. Sabino emerged.

"Hello, Molly," he said. "Is someone coming for you?"

"Yes, my brother's on his way."

"Excellent. Good job up there today with Sheila."

"Excuse me?" Maybe the principal didn't know who I was after all. "I did the talent show with Shrimp."

"That's right. Shelia O'Shea does go by Shrimp. Cute nickname for her." He chortled. "She doesn't much look like a Sheila, does she?"

Could Shrimp be the Sheila whose mom my mom had met in the bathroom at work? The girl my mom had been trying to set me up with all along? Was that even possible?

"Enjoy your weekend." He turned his attention to the new family. "Welcome to Hillsbury Middle School. I'm the principal, Mark Sabino." He thrust out his hand to shake with the parents.

The girl's eyes clouded with nervousness. I smiled at her. She smiled tightly back. I wished I could tell her not to worry. I would, I decided. I'd go right up to her on her first day.

The way Shrimp had welcomed me.

Mr. Sabino moved the group closer to the door. I edged my way to the other side of the planter and searched the long driveway for Alex's car. No brother in sight.

"And this is Roseann Bleeker," Mr. Sabino said. "Roseann is one of our special student ambassadors."

Roseann appeared at his side. Her green star pin gleamed from the pink crew neck sweater she'd pulled over her black tank. The preppy pink sweater made the outfit so much more Roseannlike.

"Hi, I'm Roseann." Her voice was bright and perky.

"I'm Avani," the girl said quietly.

I felt Avani drawn to Roseann's warm smile. She couldn't help herself. Roseann had the sparkle. I listened in fascination as Mr. Sabino gave Avani and her parents the same speech he'd given me and Mom weeks earlier.

"Why don't we come inside and go over Avani's schedule?" he suggested. The parents followed him into the school. Avani lingered a moment alongside Roseann.

"You were really good out there," Roseann said suddenly. She looked directly at me. Her blue eyes showed no anger.

"Thanks." I hesitated. "You guys were too. The dance really came together. And you looked so pretty."

"Thanks." She also hesitated.

"Listen, I didn't mean to keep hiccupping." I fiddled with my silver ring.

"I know."

"I didn't mean any of it," I said.

"I know." She turned to Avani. "This is Molly Larsen."

"Hey!" I greeted Avani.

"We need to get inside," Roseann said. "Avani, you're going to love our school. And definitely sit with me tomorrow at lunch."

Relief flooded Avani's face. "Are you sure?"

"Sure I'm sure. You look like you could use a friend at lunch. Maybe we even have a class together. Let's go see." Roseann ushered her through the door.

I stayed behind on the pathway, going over Roseann's offer to Avani. The same offer she had made to me when I didn't have a partner in social studies that scary first day. Did Roseann do this because of the green star on her sweater? Or was she just kind?

I hoped it was the latter, but I decided I didn't care.

Roseann and I would never be the best of friends. I could finally see that now. I'd had to work way too hard. I wasn't upset, though. Not at Roseann. She gave me a group and a place to sit at lunch, which was a big deal. If I was upset at anyone, it was myself. Why had I thought I could plan a friendship? Friendship should just happen, without steps and strategy sessions.

I had to tell Eden. Our plan had been flawed from the very beginning.

I hoisted my duffel onto one shoulder and my book

bag onto the other as I spotted Mom's gray car pull in with Alex at the wheel. He slowed, then stopped at the curb. I reached for the door handle.

Chrissy Bleeker sat in the passenger seat.

I whirled around to look for Roseann. Were we taking her home too?

She wasn't outside. Why was beautiful, popular Chrissy in my shy, awkward brother's car?

Chrissy rolled down her window, and Alex called, "You coming or what?"

"Hi, Molly," Chrissy greeted me. Like her sister, she wore a preppy pink sweater, and her hair hung over one shoulder in a long, loose braid.

I slid into the backseat and eyed Chrissy uncertainly.

Alex reached to shift the gears into drive and slyly touched Chrissy's hand. She didn't flinch or jerk away. Instead, she smiled at him.

"Okay, what's going on?" I demanded.

"What do you mean?" Alex pulled away from the curb, both hands now firmly on the wheel.

I poked my body forwards, stretching my head in between them. "Where are we taking Chrissy?"

"Alex is giving me a ride home," Chrissy said.

"But first we're driving you to the airport," Alex added. "I can't believe you're going. We just got here."

"You're coming with us to the airport?" I asked Chrissy.

Her cheeks turned faintly pink. "If that's okay. Alex and I were going to grab something to eat after we bring you to the gate."

"Hey, maybe we'll fly off somewhere. You know, pick a random place," Alex joked to Chrissy.

"I pick Paris. Do you like Paris?" Chrissy asked.

"Yeah, sure, totally," Alex replied. "I'd go there."

"You're not going to Paris," I told him.

"You never know." Alex's goofy grin was back. "Maybe we'll fly off. Travel the world. Eat foreign foods."

Chrissy smiled at him, as if he were saying something really funny. She liked him!

"Is this a date?" I demanded. "Did you make my airport drop-off into a first date?"

"Ignore her," Alex told Chrissy.

"It's not a *first* date," Chrissy admitted quietly.

"Whoa!" I widened my eyes at Alex. "So you two? When?"

"We met first at the library. He was studying at a table next to mine. We talked some more that day he picked you up at the park," Chrissy supplied. "Then we got together at the library a bunch of times after that."

"I thought you were going there to study!" I swatted Alex's shoulder.

"I was helping Chrissy with world history." Alex smiled broadly now.

"Your brother's supersmart." Chrissy smiled back at him.

"Eyes on the road," I reminded my brother. Settling back, I couldn't get over that Alex had found a girlfriend. Not any girlfriend, but Chrissy Bleeker! I'd never seen him so happy.

If I hadn't gone after Roseann to be my friend, I realized, Alex might never have met Chrissy on the field hockey sidelines. Pretty cool!

"Don't ever complain about driving me again," I teased him. "I got you two together."

"Did I complain today? I'm driving you all the way to Newark airport!" Nothing would shatter Alex's good mood now that Chrissy sat by his side.

Chrissy fiddled with the radio, and I stayed silent for a while, thinking.

"Alex," I said, suddenly making up my mind, "I don't want to go."

"What?"

"It's too soon," I said.

"So no airport?" he asked, gazing at me in the

rearview mirror. "Are you sure?"

"No airport," I agreed. "Not this weekend. Maybe next month."

Visiting Arizona happy instead of escaping there because I was sad would be so much better, I realized. I was just beginning to figure out my world here.

"Mom and Dad are going to be surprised," Alex said.

"Eden too," I added.

"Got to make a U-turn." Alex switched lanes. "Sorry, Chrissy, we can't do Paris today."

"That's okay. I have a field hockey game tonight anyway. There's a crepe place in the strip mall by Andover Boulevard," she said. "We could do that. It's kind of like Paris, if you don't sit by the window and see the parking lot."

"I love crepes," Alex said.

I snorted. My brother had never eaten a crepe in his life.

"I'm dropping you home, Molly. You need to call Mom and Dad," Alex said.

"About that." I popped my head between Alex and Chrissy again. "Andover Boulevard is near Top Flight, right? How about you drop me off at the gym instead?"

"You're going back there?" Alex sounded surprised.

"There's something I need to do."

"I'm not a taxi service." Alex's grumbling had returned. "I'm taking you home. Chrissy and I are going out."

"Pretty please?" I begged.

"Why don't you drop her off and then pick her up after we have our crepes?" Chrissy suggested.

"Okay, fine," Alex agreed. Anything for Chrissy!

"Thank you," I mouthed to her. A girlfriend for Alex would be good for me too, I decided. Especially a girlfriend as nice as Chrissy.

I waited by the door with the sign TOP FLIGHT GYMNASTICS until Alex and Chrissy drove off. Once I was sure they were out of sight, I shouldered my duffel bag and walked across the parking lot.

I wasn't going back to Andre's gym. My good-bye yesterday had been final.

At the opposite end of the huge warehouse building, I found what I was looking for. Another door.

Another door with a small sign.

TOP FLIGHT CHEER.

I pulled open the door and stepped inside. The roar of the cheerleaders was deafening and thrilling. For a moment, I hung back, taking it all in. The bright lights. The tumbling. The stunts. The formations. The excitement.

"Move on up . . . up to the top . . . move on up . . ." A familiar chant started nearby. A group of girls my age stood in a line, clapping and stomping their feet to the rhythm. The tall cheer coach rapped her hand against a clipboard to keep the beat. She wore the same orange warm-up jacket.

I hummed along without realizing it. Then I began to chant too. "Move on up . . . up to the top."

Shrimp stood at the end of the line. When she spotted me, she snuck a wave with her pinkie. The cheer coach caught her. She turned towards the door and noticed me.

Oh no! This wasn't such a good idea, I thought. I didn't want to get Shrimp in trouble.

"Hello again." The coach came to stand in front of me. "Using the front door today, I see."

"Yeah." I craned my neck to look up at her, realizing how truly tall she was. "I didn't mean to bother anyone."

"One more time, girls," she called over her shoulder when the cheering stopped. She completely blocked my view of Shrimp. "No red leotard, either."

"Nope." I wasn't going to say anything more, but then I noticed the skin around her eyes crinkling as she smiled down at me. My mom's eyes did that too. "That gym wasn't the right place for me," I blurted out. "I'm done. Well, if my mom can get her money back."

"Want to try some pom-poms today? We've got a spare pair. One size fits all."

"Really? Yes!" I beamed up at her. "Cheering looks like so much fun."

"Fun, sure. Hard work, definitely."

"When something's hard, I work harder," I promised.

"My kind of girl! What's your name?"

I told her, and she turned to the squad. "Molly's going to watch and learn with us today. And tomorrow, we hope she'll be back." Then she leaned down and whispered in my ear. "If you like it, Andre owns both the gymnastics and the cheering gym. Your mom won't lose any money."

"I'll be back," I told her. "You can count on it."

"Water break!" she called to the squad.

"I have shorts and sneakers in my bag." I pointed to the duffel I'd dropped at my feet.

"I like a girl who travels with possibilities. A girl who opens new doors." She nodded to the far wall. "You know where the locker room is. Change, then come show me some pep."

I hurried inside. My overstuffed bag had certainly come in handy today. Who knew throwing everything from my closet into the bag made me such a good packer?

"I knew it! I knew it!" Shrimp burst into the locker room. "I knew you should be a cheerleader."

"I can't wait to tumble with you." I pulled on my shorts and tied my sneakers.

"You and me, Christmas tree." She jumped up and down with excitement.

"Um, that one didn't work so well."

"I know, right?" Shrimp wrinkled her freckled nose. "Help me here? I need a better rhyme."

"Tennessee? Or how about bumblebee?"

"I like that. You and me, bumblebee." Shrimp buzzed loudly in my ear.

I buzzed even louder in hers. She buzzed back. Soon we couldn't stop laughing.

"Listen. Is your real name Sheila?" I asked.

"Yuck. Don't ever repeat that. It's a secret." She narrowed her eyes. "How did you dig up my horrible name?"

"I think my mom met your mom in the bathroom where they work. Weird, right?"

"Totally," Shrimp agreed.

Then I had an idea. "Since we're friends, maybe our moms can be friends too?" How great would it be if I found Mom a friend? And one who lived practically in our backyard?

"Works for me. You guys can come over tonight." Shrimp smirked. "Does she want to climb the fence?"

"I'm thinking we'll leave the sheets on your beds and walk."

After I changed, I pulled out my phone. "I need to call my friend Eden really quickly."

"Hurry," Shrimp said. "Coach doesn't like us to be late. I want to show you what we do out there."

"Don't be mad, but I'm not coming today," I told Eden when she picked up.

"Really?" The disappointment in her voice was clear. "I got a bunch of avocados for your masks. I thought we'd order burritos from Senor Chavez too."

"Yum. Oh, Eden, I'm sorry."

"Did your mom say no?" she asked.

"She was surprisingly good with it," I admitted. "Stuff came up. I'm going to hang out here and come another time. I'm really sorry."

"Roseann stuff?" Eden sounded excited for me. "Is everything great with you two now?"

"Everything's great, but not with Roseann. The best friend thing isn't going to happen with us."

"Oh no!" Eden cried. "I thought all our steps were

working. They seemed to be, right?"

"I followed our steps, but you know what? They led to the wrong girl."

"Wrong girl? What do you mean?" she asked.

"I found a different friend. A better friend. A friend who likes to have fun." I smiled at Shrimp. "You'd love her too."

"Who is she? Tell me all!" Eden gushed.

"Shrimp!" I said. "I'll call you later with all the details, okay? Right now I'm going to learn how to be a cheerleader."

"Cheerleader?" Eden cried. "Whoa!"

"Lots of changes here," I told her. "Good ones."

"Hi, Eden!" Shrimp called.

"Is that her?" Eden asked.

"That is. Wait a sec. I'm sending you a photo."

Flipping my phone, I focused in on me and Shrimp. We squished our faces together as I snapped our photo. Then I snapped another, making fishy faces. And another with wide eyes.

I sent them to Eden.

My kind of It Girl! I texted.

Eden texted back: ☺

READ ON FOR A SNEAK PEEK
OF PICTURE PERFECT #2,

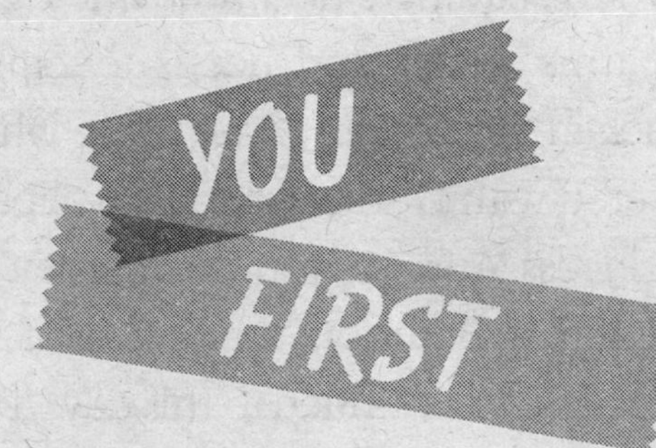

Finn slipped a hair elastic off her wrist and pulled her shoulder-length blond hair into a low ponytail. "Okay," she said, narrowing her eyes. "Party planning. Let's do this."

Gigi couldn't help but laugh. Of course Finn would approach their task with the same intensity as a big soccer match. Of course she would.

"What we need," Finn continued, "is a strategy."

Gigi shook her head. "What we need is the Wall."

The two of them turned to face the wall opposite Gigi's loft bed. It was fourteen feet of history between them. Every last inch had been covered with posters, pictures, stickers, pages ripped from magazines—if you could stick it somewhere, the Wall was where it went.

Finley had actually started the tradition, with

a picture of the two of them taken on the first day of preschool. They were dressed in matching blue jumpers and red-sequined flats, and they grinned at the camera, arms linked and heads touching. She'd pasted it smack in the center of the Wall, which at the time was covered with Disney princess wallpaper. Finn declared, "Princess Aurora, you are hereby banished from the Kingdom of Bedroom. Long live Eff and Gee!"

It was a ritual they continued to this day, "banishing" the things they'd outgrown, like the sparkly Polly Pocket decal and a poster of a certain boy band of brothers. Whatever replaced the "banished" item was proclaimed to be superior—the best, coolest, most Eff and Gee thing *ever*.

Sometimes the ceremonies were solemn, like when they'd come down with a serious case of Bieber fever. Other times, they were beyond silly, like when they took turns replacing the heads of My Little Ponies with those of their favorite celebrities. Like centaurs, but with famous people. (Together Eff and Gee had declared, "Long live the cen-stars!")

There was the photo of last year's *The Cat in the Hat*—with Gigi in costume and makeup as the titular feline, and Finn decked out as Thing One—pasted among souvenirs from every other play and talent show

Gigi and Finn had ever been in.

Another section of the Wall was devoted entirely to birthday parties past; each year, the girls cut the number of their age out of theme-appropriate scrapbook paper and pasted a picture of themselves from the party on top of it.

There was last year's mall scavenger hunt, of course. For their tenth birthday blowout, they'd thrown a retro roller skating party at the Christiana Skating Center. For nine, they both dressed up as Hermione Granger for their Harry Potter party, and two years before that was the karaoke slumber party they had in Finley's basement. They'd invited so many girls, you couldn't so much as walk to the bathroom without stepping on someone's sleeping bag.

Gigi's eyes rested on her favorite photo of the bunch—the super-glam portrait of her and Finn from their sixth birthday party, which had been held at a Sweet & Sassy salon in neighboring Pennsylvania. Because of the distance, their parents had rented them an honest-to-goodness pink limo, and all of their best girlfriends piled in. The only grown-ups allowed were Gigi's and Finley's moms. Technically, Finley's little brother, Logan, had been on board too, as he'd hitched a ride in Finn's mother's swollen belly.

"Remember how much fun that was?" Gigi asked, running her finger along the photo's glittery pink frame.

"Aww," Finn cooed. "Look how cute we are in those matching sequined tutus!"

"Whatever we decide for this party," Gigi said, "I feel strongly that it should include costumes."

Finn sighed. "Not everyone likes to play dress-up, Gee."

"But *we* do," Gigi responded. "And it's *our* birthday. So. If our friends want to bask in our fabulousness, they're going to have to dress appropriately."

Finley nodded like she agreed but then started to nibble on an invisible hangnail on her thumb. This, Gigi knew, was something her best friend did when she was conflicted. A nervous habit, born out of the fact that Finn hated to argue about anything.

Now it was Gigi's turn to sigh. Why wouldn't Finley just talk to her? How hard was it to tell your best friend what you were really thinking?

Then, as if she had read Gigi's mind, Finley said, "It's just that . . . well, costumes are more your thing than mine. So couldn't we, um, make them optional?"

"Of course," Gigi said. "As long as they stay on the menu. Deal?"

Finley grinned. "Deal."

The girls continued to bat ideas back and forth. Or rather, Gigi batted ideas to Finn, who proceeded to shoot them down.

GEE: What about a Southern tea party? We could have finger sandwiches and—ooh!—I can ask my mom-mom to make her famous seven-layer coconut cake!

EFF: Tea party? I thought we were turning twelve, not a hundred and twelve.

GEE: (Thinking.)

EFF: (Staring at same invisible hangnail.)

GEE: I know! We can go full-on Peter Pan, complete with pirate treasure hunt.

EFF: (Shoots Gee a look.)

GEE: What? You wanted something younger!

EFF: Maybe not that young.

GEE: Okayyy. How about a super-cool Las Vegas theme? We could play poker—with M&Ms, of course.

EFF: Of course.

GEE: It could be really swanky. Ooh! We can make the invitations out of playing cards!

EFF: Huh.

GEE: What?

EFF: Southern tea? Steel Magnolias. Peter Pan? Hook. Vegas? Ocean's Eleven. Do you have any birthday party ideas not inspired by a Julia Roberts movie?

GEE: What's wrong with Julia Roberts?

EFF: Nothing. I'm just saying, our party doesn't have to have some kind of tie to your redheaded spirit twin.

[END BRAINSTORM SESSION.]

Gigi flopped back on her bed, covering her face with her arms. "This is hopeless!" she cried. "We're getting nowhere."

"True," Finn agreed. "You know what we need? A break."

"A break from what?"

"We're thinking way too hard about this. I say we go downstairs, make a couple of smoothies, and watch a movie. I'll even let you pick which one."

"Even if it's *Runaway*—"

"*Bride*," Finn finished for her. "Yes. I had a feeling you'd go for that one."

And just that like that, Gigi felt the party-planning tension melt clean away.

As the closing credits rolled, Finn put her sneakers back on and tightened the laces.

"Are you leaving?" Gigi asked.

"It'll be getting dark soon," Finley said. "I need to

finish my run."

"But what about the party?"

"Tomorrow," Finn said. "After cooking class. I promise we'll figure it out then. 'Kay?"

Gigi nodded. She wasn't sure why she felt quite so deflated. It must've shown on her face, though, because Finn said, "Don't look so mopey. We'll get this party planned. We always do." Finn waved as she jogged out the door. "It's the weekend. We'll have plenty of time. Thank *god* it's Friday, right, dude?"

Finn headed out the door, and Gigi trudged back upstairs to her room.

It was just shy of five, which meant it was almost eleven in Prague. Her father's company had sent him there earlier in the week, but work had kept him so busy they'd only Skyped once, instead of every day like they usually did on his extended business trips.

At her desk, Gigi fired up her laptop. She launched Skype and clicked to connect with GeorgePrince71, but he didn't answer. *This is exactly why,* she thought, *her mother simply had to get her an iPhone for her birthday.* That way she could just text her father, like any normal girl her age.

Disconnected from her dad. Ditched by her BFF.

TGIF? Gigi thought. *Yeah, right.*

READY FOR A PICTURE-PERFECT FRIENDSHIP?

Gigi Stewart and her best friend, Finley, are always together. But when Gigi suggests they start planning their annual joint birthday blowout, Finn doesn't seem that into it.

Gigi thought she and Finn would be friends forever—but what happens when "forever" comes to an end?

HARPER
An Imprint of HarperCollins*Publishers*

www.harpercollinschildrens.com